Reunion at Red Paint Bay

Reunion

at

Red Paint Bay

GEORGE HARRAR

OTHER PRESS
New York

Production Editor: Yvonne E. Cárdenas
Book design: Jennifer Daddio/Bookmark Design & Media, Inc.
Title page photo: Joe Duraes
This book was set in 11.75 pt Cochin
by Alpha Design & Composition of Pittsfield, NH.

1 3 5 7 9 10 8 6 4 2

Library of Congress Cataloging-in-Publication Data

Harrar, George, 1949–
Reunion at Red Paint Bay / by George Harrar.
p. cm.
ISBN 978-1-59051-545-7 (trade pbk.) — ISBN 978-1-59051-546-4 (e-book)
1. Journalists—Fiction.   2. Stalkers—Fiction.   3. Rape—
Fiction.   4. Maine—Fiction.   5. Domestic fiction.   I. Title.
PS3558.A624924R48 2013
813'.54—dc23
2012003130

TO LINDA
my wife and personal editor

'Tis a pleasant thing, from the shore,
to behold the drowning of another . . . not
because it is a grateful pleasure for
anyone to be in misery, but because it is
a pleasant thing to see those misfortunes
from which you yourself are free.

–LUCRETIUS

Reunion at Red Paint Bay

One

RED PAINT
Pop. 7,142
Friendliest Town in Maine

Simon Howe, editor of the *Red Paint Register*, drove south toward home, into the fading light. Beyond the rusting town sign, as far as one could see into the scrub pine woods, there was no other imprint on the land to suggest what lay ahead. A sign wasn't really necessary. People didn't just happen upon Red Paint. If you took the spur road off the interstate, you probably already lived there and knew where you were going. Simon reached over the gearshift and let his hand fall on the knee of his wife, Amy. She had been quiet for miles, unusual for her, all the way from their dinner at the Bayswater Inn. Maybe she was worrying about their son, home alone for the first time. If there was separation anxiety, he figured it was more on her part than Davey's.

A small flash of light in the brush caught his eye as he approached the train tracks. He stopped as if the wooden barrier arms were down and felt the night breeze dampening his face, bringing with it the faintly dank smell of the marshes. "Lightning bugs," he said, "there were always hundreds of them in our yard in summer when I was a kid. I used to snatch them from the air and put them in a glass jar. It was like catching fire."

Amy followed his gaze into the woods to see what he was seeing. "Maybe that's why they're disappearing, all the little boys putting them in jars."

Simon stared into the tall weeds for a minute, watching for another flicker, but there was none. He drove on, the old Toyota rattling across the tracks and straining up the steep hill. At the top the length and breadth of Red Paint, four miles by three, stretched out ahead of them. It appeared like a watercolor of a town, a still life at dusk. There was no main road, just a narrow ribbon of asphalt snaking from the cottages on the bay to the bungalows dotting the eastern pine woods. In between lay the town center, an irregular common of grass bordered by brick storefronts. In the middle, a red-and-black bandstand, dated 1813. From its steps, visiting politicians invariably praised the good citizens of Red Paint for sticking to their roots. Staying put turned into a virtue.

"How many people do you think will show?" she asked.

"Where?"

"Your reunion. Think they'll fill the ballroom?"

"I don't know. I hate reunions. It's like turning into your own embarrassing teenage self again for a night."

"I'm looking forward to it, meeting your old sweethearts."

"I had girlfriends, not sweethearts." Ginnie, Nora, Lauren—he hadn't thought of them in years. Except Ginnie, once in a while.

Amy tapped his arm. "I forgot. I promised Davey we'd bring him a cheeseburger and fries for staying alone."

Simon glanced in the rearview mirror before slowing. "He didn't need an incentive. He practically shoved us out the door."

"He was putting up a good front. I know he was nervous."

Simon did a U-turn into the dusty parking lot at Red's Diner, circled the flashing *RED'S* sign, and pulled back onto Route 7, Bayswater Road.

Amy angled the air vent toward her face. "So," she said, "what are you leading with this week?"

She often asked this. Sometimes he made up absurd stories of UFO sightings over Red Paint Bay or terrorist groups training out by the old gravel pits to avoid mentioning what always filled page one—tedious articles about variance applications and town meeting procedures. Tonight he just wasn't in the mood to pretend. "I suppose I'll play up that guy who lost his toe in the landfill accident last month. He's filed suit against the town. I was thinking of the headline *Big Toe Worth $500K?*"

"Provocative question."

"Right. The city papers will be all over it for follow-ups."

He came up fast on a turning car, and Amy stiffened against her seat as he veered onto the gravel shoulder, then back onto solid road. He drove past Black Bear Miniature Golf and Ten-Pin Alley, neither with any visible signs of life. What were the other 7,140 citizens of Red Paint doing in their houses at this hour, watching some alternative reality on TV? "I was thinking of a new tagline for the *Register*," he said, "*Nothing Happens—And We Report It.*"

"Catchy."

"It's actually the slogan for a Buddhist newspaper, so it's much deeper than it seems." Two bright lights came up quickly in the rearview mirror, white disks, then turned off abruptly, as if disappearing into the woods. He kept watching, expecting a police car to appear, blue lights flashing in hot pursuit. He would turn around and follow, of course, just like in his reporter days in Portland. He saw nothing. "You know when the last murder was in Red Paint?"

Amy took a long drink from her water bottle. "It must have been before we bought the house—at least ten years."

"Twenty years ago this week, a biker was shot outside the Mechanic Pub. All that time since without a killing."

"You sound disappointed."

Maybe he was. A murder focused the mind of a small town as no other event could. A murder could make people feel like victims and ask what the world was coming to. A murder could make them lock their doors at night. And, of course, people bought papers to read every grisly detail. "It's just surprising," he said. "You figure somebody would pick up a loose .22 once in a while to settle an argument."

The giant Burger World sign came into view, and Amy braced one hand against the dashboard. He turned into the takeout lane with exaggerated slowness, inched up to the large plastic ear, and leaned out the window. "One cheeseburger, well done, and regular fries."

"Would you like to maxi-size your order for another dollar, sir?" The voice was gentle and soft, a young girl's voice that he hadn't heard before. She sounded pretty to him, but he couldn't say why. He considered making up some reason to go inside to see, a test of his intuition.

"Sir?"

"Yes. I mean no."

"Okay," the sweet voice said, "that will be $3.74. Please pull up to the next window. And have a nice night."

As the Toyota crept forward Amy ducked her head into the middle of the car and called out, "Thank you," which seemed unnecessary to him, since she wasn't part of the transaction. But harmless. Just Amy.

"You know . . . ," she said, settling back into her seat.

"What?"

"It wouldn't hurt for you to be more friendly with people."

"Which people?"

"The girl back there."

He glanced over his shoulder. "You want me to be more friendly ordering a cheeseburger and fries from a giant clown's ear?"

"You can be terse sometimes."

"I'm succinct, not terse. The teenager inside that ear or wherever she is could care less as long as I order quickly. They run on volume here, not friendliness." Simon took a five-dollar bill out of his wallet. "Does this have anything to do with the FRIENDLIEST TOWN sign? Because you realize that was just a marketing ploy. The Downtown Association dreamed it up to lure small businesses."

"I've just noticed you can sound unpleasant with people. They could get the wrong impression."

"Unpleasant?" He backed the car down the narrow drive-thru lane and stopped alongside the yellow ear. "Excuse me. Hello?"

"Would you like to change your order, sir?"

"No, I just wanted to ask, when I ordered, did I sound terse to you?"

"Terse?"

He wondered about the word—was it above the comprehension level of a teenager working at Burger World? "Terse or rude," he said, aiming his words into the bright lemon ear canal. "Was I unpleasant?"

"No, you were okay. You should hear some of the guys. They're pretty gross."

Simon rested his arm out the window. "I'm sorry you have to listen to that."

"Yeah, for seven bucks an hour. But I can get back at them, if I want."

He pictured her red-painted fingernails grinding roaches into a paste to spread over the burger and squeezing out a dirty sponge into a Coke. A horn blew from behind. "Well," Simon said, "good luck."

"Thanks. Your order's ready now."

At the pickup window a teenaged boy handed out the black-and-white BW bag, with the familiar grinning cow face on the side. Simon looked in. "She gave us extra ketchup. Lots of it." As he pulled away he twisted back to call out "Thank you" to the bulky kid, who smiled and waved.

The car bumped along Crescent Street, Red Paint's perpetually torn-up road, as Amy squeezed a perfect line of ketchup onto a French fry. He always marveled at how steady her hand was. He wondered how many fries she would eat. Invariably he underestimated. She said, "Did you hire your replacement for the press-room yet?"

"Didn't I tell you? The guy was in the Red Sox farm system for a while then worked at the *Portland Press Herald*." Simon turned on the radio. "That reminds me, the game should be on."

The station was always tricky to dial in this far up the coast, and static filled the air. Amy touched the knob to tune the channel better. "How did you lure him to the *Register*, promise a drastic pay cut?"

"He left there seven years ago."

"Where's he worked since?"

It was a helpful trait for a psychiatric therapist to be curious, as his wife was by nature, pushing every odd bit of information to the bitter end in case it held some unforeseen significance. But in normal conversation he found this habit irritating. Some topics were left unfin-ished for a reason.

"He hasn't really worked."

"What's he been doing since leaving the *Press Herald*?"

Simon thought of the claim the man had made dur-ing the interview—that he had read more than a hun-dred books in the past year. Mostly crime fiction, but still. "He's been reading a lot, two books a week."

Amy ate another of Davey's French fries. "Who has time to read that much?"

"Retired people, the sick, the unemployed, people without TVs or kids."

"Which is he?"

The option was there for him to pick. But one lie would necessarily lead to another, as Amy pursued his story. "Actually, a prisoner."

She rolled up the top of the Burger World bag. "He was in jail?"

"Still is, up in Warren. His release date's tomorrow."

"What did he do?"

Simon didn't want to say. He didn't really know anyway, not specifically, at least. "I probably shouldn't be talking about this."

She reached over and poked his neck. "Come on, spill it."

"Okay, he assaulted a woman."

Amy lifted her arm from his shoulder, the understanding instantaneous. "He raped her?"

Simon drove.

"You hired a rapist?"

The description seemed so all-encompassing, as if a single word could sum up a man's whole nature rather than just one awful act. Didn't a person deserve at least a few sentences about his life before being judged?

"I assume he didn't put that on his résumé," Amy said.

"He had a record, not a résumé."

She glanced out of the window, then back at him. "You didn't tell me you were thinking of hiring a rapist."

"I didn't know I was. I just went up there to check out the new incentives the state has for hiring prisoners when they're released. I ended up doing some interviews."

"And hiring a rapist."

"As it turned out."

"There weren't any pedophiles or murderers available?"

Simon braked hard at Five Corners, even though normally he would take his chances coasting through on the yellow to avoid waiting through the multiple lights. "I sense you don't approve."

"I'm just wondering why you would hire a rapist."

Rapist—how many times would she say it? "This guy has a name, which is David Rigero, and David scored higher than most of our regular applicants on the employment test. I liked him, too."

"Liked him how?"

"As someone to talk to. If I were sitting next to him on an airplane, I'd enjoy our conversation."

"You're planning trips with him?"

"No," he answered, even knowing she was being facetious. "But it's a small office, and I prefer to like the people I hire. He wants to do some stringing for us, too. He has an aptitude for writing."

The traffic crept by in front of them—a few cars, a gasoline tanker, and a white unmarked truck, the kind often mentioned on crime reports as spotted leaving the scene. Should the people inside these vehicles all be judged by the worst thing they had ever done? Who could survive that scrutiny?

"So," she said, "whose life did this wonderful conversationalist of yours ruin?"

Simon debated with himself for a moment making up a name. *Sally Jenkins* popped into his head. It sounded believable. "I didn't ask."

"You weren't curious about his victim?"

"What would a name tell me? I didn't ask him anything specific about what he's in for. It didn't seem appropriate." Simon waited for a woman carrying two bags of groceries to cross in front of the Toyota, then pulled carefully through Five Corners. It was the most dangerous intersection in Red Paint.

"Maybe she could use a job," Amy said. For a moment he thought she meant the woman crossing the street. "That is, if she's gotten over the trauma of being sexually assaulted by your new hire."

Simon accelerated quickly, and the rattle started up again. Amy whacked the dashboard with the heel of her hand.

"You might trigger the air bag that way."

She pounded harder with her fist. "At least it would stop the goddamn rattle."

He took her hand in his. "I'm sorry, okay? I wouldn't have hired the guy if I knew you would react so strongly." He said this clearly, no qualifications. It was easy to apologize for something he didn't have any intention of changing. "I thought I was doing good here, giving a second chance to a person who's paid his debt to society."

She started to say something, then thought for a moment. "You know that half my practice is women who have been abused in some way. I hear their stories every day. Their abusers get out of jail after a few years and move on—and those are the ones who even get convicted. The women never escape, especially from rape."

"So David Rigero should be locked up forever, throw away the key? Or let him out with no job and no future?"

"I didn't say that. But you didn't have to hire him."

"Right, I should have just let him pick from all the other job offers he had."

They rode on in silence. Amy rarely let arguments die out like this, with his getting the last word. He wished it would happen more often. In a few minutes he turned onto Fox Run and into their driveway. He switched off the engine and opened his door. She stayed in her seat, holding the Burger World bag. He never realized how idiotic the grinning cow looked.

"Coming?" he said.

She looked over at him. "I never want to meet this man, Simon."

He nodded. But Red Paint was a small town. It was impossible to say that any two people might not meet some day.

Two

By *tradition the editor* of the *Register* sat at the original oak desk facing the arching window that overlooked Mechanic Street and the tree-lined Common. When he bought the paper ten years ago Simon Greenleaf Howe did as his predecessors for the last century, letting anyone who wanted see into the offices, day or night.

He sat alone now in the editorial room late Tuesday, production day. The overhead fluorescent lights swayed in the stiff currents of air coming from two floor-size fans in opposite corners. There was the faint hum of the large air conditioning units from the municipal offices next door. Otherwise not a sound. He felt groggy, as if overwhelmed by some sleep-inducing aerosol injected into the office. He rubbed his eyes, trying to bring focus to the page-one proof on his desk and the last-minute story that needed his attention.

Mother and Child Saved
from Fiery Crash
by Ellen Collins

Randall Caine admits he's an impulsive man. Fortunately for one little girl, the auto mechanic didn't think twice when he saw the Chevy Malibu in front of him skid off Dakin Road and burst into flames Monday evening. The 27-year-old Caine literally jumped into the fire to rescue a battered and bruised Viola Lang, age 5.

The driver, Jennifer Lang, 29, was able to crawl from the burning wreck on her own. Mother and child are recuperating at Bayview Hospital in stable condition. The car and its contents were destroyed, except for a pair of lucky dice hanging from the rearview mirror, which were thrown clear during the spinout.

Firemen from the Northside Firehouse were practicing ladder techniques in Portland that day and arrived at the scene only in time to douse the smoldering car. For his bravery, Caine is being hailed as "the hero of Dakin Road" by Mayor Joseph Samuels, who later this week . . .

(continued on page 8)

15

Simon pictured the scene—Randy Caine in his blood red RAISIN' CAINE AUTO PARTS T-shirt plunging into the fire to save a little girl. Randy wasn't a guy to hesitate while considering consequences. There probably weren't any consequences worth considering in his world. There was just plunging into the fire or not. This time he plunged. Simon circled the headline with his black marker and wrote, "Inc to 36 pt." In the body of the story he crossed out *literally*. How else could a person jump? He drew a line through the whole Northside Firehouse sentence. There was no need to portray the local firemen as practicing at their job while a car burned. It would gall them enough that a Caine, not exactly the first family of Red Paint, was being lauded for courage. The town rowdy had become a hero, and what was Mayor Samuels to do, give Randy a Get Out of Jail Free card? No doubt he would need it soon enough. Simon drew a star in the margin at the dice being thrown clear during the spinout, as if luck had saved them from cremation. It was the kind of quirky detail the *Register* was known for.

He scanned the rest of the proof. *Man Sues Town Over Landfill Mishap* read the lead headline, and underneath: *Big Toe Worth $500K?* A provocative question indeed. Just below the fold, a grip-and-grin shot of First Red Paint Bank president John DeMonico handing out twenty-year service medals was cropped so tightly that the recipients looked like smiling heads on a platter. Simon scribbled, "These people have necks, don't they? Recrop." In a small box next to the picture was the headline *25th Reunion*. He had run the notice for the last month, a recurring reminder of his own impending milestone. He could anticipate the question from classmates he hadn't seen in decades—*What happened, Simon? You're the last person I expected to get trapped in Red Paint.* The boy the yearbook had declared *Most Likely to Go to Mars* now owned the only newspaper in town and lived just a mile from the house he grew up in. There was his name on the last line of the box. *Simon Howe—Reunion Publicity.* It was hard to explain, even to himself.

His eyes drifted to the bottom right corner of page one and The Weekly Quotation: *"Humankind cannot bear very much reality"* —*T. S. Eliot.* "Intriguing choice, Barb," he wrote to his newly divorced editorial assistant, "but how about something a little more up-beat next week?" That was it, another edition ready for press with barely a glimmer of hard news. On the positive side, he had stretched copy and enlarged pictures to cover all thirty-two pages. It was an achievement worth noting, but to whom? Did Pulitzer give an award for filling space?

Simon dialed the pressroom, then cradled the phone at his neck as he pulled on his jacket. "I'm done marking up page one, Meg," he said. "I'll leave it on my desk." A few moments later the rear door opened, and *the rapist* came in. How else could he think of him? It was the first time Simon had seen his new hire at the office. Rigero's hair was trimmed to the scalp on the sides and his mustache was shaved off, which made him look ten years younger. But instead of seeming like a younger version of himself, he looked like an entirely different person, a complete change of face. It unnerved Simon a little to try to match up the image in his mind with the man in front of him.

"Ms. Locklear sent me for the proof, Mr. Howe. She's on paste-up."

Simon didn't recognize the voice, either. It was lighter, with a kind of smoothness to the tone, nothing halting or clipped.

"Mr. Howe?"

Simon held out page one. "Here it is, David."

Rigero stared at the lead headline. "Kind of strange."

"What's that?"

"If a big toe's worth a half a million, how much would fingers go for, or like a head or something?"

"I don't know of any blue book of body parts," Simon said. "They're worth whatever a jury says."

Rigero held out his left hand in a fist and opened his fingers one at a time, as if counting up how much each one could bring.

There was something about Davey that seemed odd to Simon lately. The boy hadn't grown noticeably.

His hair was the same—gelled up to make him appear taller. His voice didn't have any hint of adolescent timbre to it yet. He still dashed and crashed around the house, still curled up on the couch between them watching a movie on Friday evenings, still wanted to be read to at night and tickled to get out of bed in the morning. But there was an added dimension to all these things, something unfamiliar just below the facade. Like at this moment, standing in the driveway with an object in his hand, staring into the backyard. His chin was slightly turned up, inclining his gaze to the trees. Simon watched him for a minute and was amazed at how motionless the boy could be when he wanted to. Not a trace of hyperactivity. But what could make him want to stay so still? Simon pulled back from the kitchen window, went to the side door, and stepped outside. Davey's hand was empty now. He was looking at his feet.

"What's up, buddy?"

"Nothing."

Simon moved closer, trying to detect any bulge in a pocket or shirt that might hint at the hidden item. Then he saw the drawing on the front of Davey's shirt, white on black, small skeletons floating in the air. He reached out and grabbed a bit of the cloth.

Davey jumped back. "What are you doing?"

Simon pulled the bottom taut, exposing the words— DEAD BABIES. "Where'd you get this?"

The boy looked down at his chest. "I don't know. I've had it for like forever."

"Mom didn't buy it for you?"

Davey shook his head. "I buy my own stuff."

"With our money."

"What am I supposed to do, get a job to pay for clothes?"

The tone was combative, as so often lately, but Simon wouldn't take the bait. "A paper route wouldn't hurt," he said. "You could earn your spending money."

"Sorry, Dad, but the only paper in town pays kids three bucks an hour."

"Plus tips." Simon stared at the odd expression on the dead babies, as if they were in a blissful state of nonexistence. It wasn't a gory depiction at all. Still, not appropriate. "I don't want you wearing that to school."

The boy kicked the toe of his sneaker into the ground, sending up a clump of grass. "The teachers don't care. They can't stop you anyway. It's like my freedom to wear what I want."

"Sorry, kiddo, but my responsibility as a parent trumps your freedom of expression. Dead babies aren't a suitable thing to be wearing on a shirt anywhere, let alone at school. And don't kick up the grass."

Davey stopped his foot in midair and set it down again. Then he put his hands on his hips, a provocative little pose. "Can I go now?"

"Sure," Simon said, and he really was happy at that moment for his son to get out of his sight.

When Amy came through the front door, he was already pouring wine in the kitchen. "You're late," he called into her, "so I started without you."

She stepped out of her shoes, leaving them in the hallway. "I had to go to an antiviolence workshop in Portland. It ran over."

He poured the Merlot to the brim, red filling her glass. It was a challenge for him, how high he could go without spilling. "Change anybody's mind from pro-violence to antiviolence?"

She took the glass in two hands and sipped, as if from a chalice. "You should realize by now your sarcasm is useless on me. It just doesn't stick."

"That's why I can be as sarcastic as I want. You don't take it personally."

Amy opened the refrigerator and pulled out a celery stalk. She swirled it in her wine, then bit off the end. "Davey upstairs?"

Simon nodded. "You know he's wearing a T-shirt with dead babies on it?"

She did seem to know. "I think it's an undead, vampire kind of thing the kids are into. I don't like it either. Maybe I'll make it disappear the next time he puts it in the wash." She turned onto the side porch and flopped on the wicker sofa. It was detox time.

"So," Simon said, sitting on the window ledge across from her. That was all he ever needed to say.

"The climax of my day was the tarantula lady. She lives in one of those new monstrosities in Bay Estates. Three thousand square feet just for herself and a dozen tarantulas."

"She keeps tarantulas?"

"She rescues ones that are injured or deformed. She's actually quite famous in spider circles. She's written books on baboon spiders, mouse spiders, bird-eating spiders."

Simon dipped the tip of his finger in the wine and ran it around the rim of the glass. It was a strangely pleasant sensation. "So why's she seeing you—a troublesome tarantula?"

"She's obsessed with observing every little event in her life like it's deeply meaningful. She's all wrapped up in memory."

"That doesn't sound so serious."

"It is for her. She never sees the big picture. She thinks her life is an accumulation of minutely analyzed experiences, and she feels compelled to relate every one of them to me."

Simon yawned at the thought of it. "I don't know how you can listen to that stuff all day. It's basically people saying, 'Aren't I a fascinating human being with all of these weird thoughts for you to interpret?'"

Amy bit off another piece of wine-soaked celery. "And you know this from what, your nonexistent first-hand experience with treatment yourself?"

"All I know about therapy I learned from you."

She wiped her lips with her hand. "At the end of the session I stood up, her cue to leave, and she says, 'I feel like I'm just getting started. I want to go for another hour.' I said, 'Let's keep to our regular schedule.' She said she'd pay me double. She was desperate to keep talking about herself and I'm thinking, This is your problem, you consume yourself focusing on every stray bit of your life. I tried reasoning with her, I tried coaxing her, I tried being forceful with her, and then I decided that was wrong, I was playing into her, so I picked up the phone. She got the message. She left."

"Good, you—"

"Wait, that's not all. I went out to my car, checked my rearview mirror, and there she was, standing right behind me. If I hadn't looked, I would have run her over."

Simon thought about the bizarre situation taking shape and the jeopardy Amy had been in. Driving over someone could never be explained, even if the victim was asking for it. "What did you do?"

"I leaned out to talk to her, but she put her hands over her ears. So I hit the horn. She left."

He hoisted his glass in the air. "Congratulations. You won."

"Therapy isn't a power struggle. I'm not supposed to induce anxiety in my patients. She surprised me, and I reacted badly."

He leaned across the space between them and gave her a kiss on her forehead. "I'm sure you'll be ready for her next time."

Three

The *message on the postcard* said: "What good are funerals? They offer no solace. If God had all possibilities in His hands at Creation, was Death really the best He could come up with as The End? Faithfully . . ."

The signature was unreadable. The first letter looked like a ragged *F* or *P*. The rest of the name ran together, a row of inverted *v*'s, like a child's drawing of waves. Simon turned the card over. Great Salt Lake was scrolled atop a borderless expanse of water. On the side hung a white bag, thumbnail size, marked Genuine GSL Salt. He rolled the bag between his fingers as he walked down the hallway and into the kitchen. Amy was at the breakfast table hammering the keys of her laptop. It was her day to enter session notes.

He waited for her to look up. "Do we know anyone who died recently in Salt Lake?"

"I don't think people drown there. You can almost sit on the water."

"I meant in the city." Simon held the card in front of her eyes.

"It does make you think," she said.

"What?"

"Why God created the kind of death we have out of all the possibilities."

"Such as?"

"He could have had everyone die at the same age, or everyone die painlessly, or have the dead reappear as spirits to reassure us they're doing okay on the other side—that one would have been especially nice."

"Maybe God created all those possibilities in other worlds. We just got the one with frequently painful death and unknown afterlife."

Amy pointed at the card. "Did you notice, this is addressed to *Master* Simon Howe."

He looked again. "I haven't been called Master since my grandmother died and stopped sending me birthday cards."

Amy reached up and squeezed the bag of salt. "Sending a tourist card from a funeral, that sounds like something one of your cousins would do."

Simon took the postcard and slid it under the bright yellow fish magnet on the refrigerator, which is where they saved all the odd things they might need later.

He stood in the semicircle of his reporters and wrote *Story Ideas* on the easel. The black marker squeaked across the paper, leaving a faint grade-school smell. Outside the window Erasmus Hall, Red Paint's resident harbinger of the apocalypse, shook a fistful of tracts at anyone passing by. "Repent!" filtered through the glass, a scratchy, almost plaintive plea. Erasmus was losing his voice.

A purposeful cough drew Simon's attention back into the newsroom. "Okay, Barbara," he said, "anything interesting from the Selectmen this week?"

His editorial assistant stood up and smoothed her black skirt down her legs. "They just faxed over the agenda," she said. "They're supposed to debate the town meeting article on the Common improvements, but Jack Harris may show up again and make a fuss about them breaking the open meeting law a couple weeks ago. They had him thrown out last time."

Simon wrote *Possible Chaos at Selectmen's Meeting.* "Sign up Ron to go with you in case Harris shows," he said. "We don't want to miss a shot of the Selectmen tossing him out the door this time." Simon turned toward Joe Armin, a young man with an inch-long pin through his left ear, which he pulled at whenever anyone was looking his way. "How's the reunion preview going?"

Joe tugged at his ear. "Don't take this wrong, chief, but your class was wicked dull. All anybody remembers is stealing the school bell and running somebody's bra up the flagpole. Maybe because it's been so long nobody can remember anything interesting."

"It was only twenty-five years ago."

Joe whistled at the thought of it. "Man, I haven't even lived that long."

It was true—no one on the staff except Barbara was within a decade in age of their editor. The paper couldn't afford to pay for maturity or experience, and why would anyone with either choose to work in Red Paint, Maine? Simon glanced at the railroad station clock jutting from the back wall as he did reflexively a half-dozen times a day, even though time was stuck there at 7:45. A.m. or p.m.? When exactly did time stop at the *Register*?

His gaze returned to the front of the room. "Check with Holly Green over at the bank, Joe. She was president of our class. She'll come up with some stories. Okay, Ellen, what do you have on the features side?"

A woman in jeans and a sleeveless yellow top straightened in her chair. "I got a call from a woman at 33 Larkspur Drive," she said, flipping through her black reporter's notebook. "Elizabeth Nichols. She says the Virgin Mary appeared in her backyard."

Ellen laughed a little, as did Simon, but no one else. "I guess none of you was here when she showed up in the freezer frost at Bay Market," he said. They looked blankly at him, confirming his assumption. "So Ellen, how has Mary chosen to incarnate herself this time?"

The reporter's face contorted, as if she were imagining herself in the Virgin's predicament. "She's sitting in a mound of dirt. The family was putting in a therapeutic spa for their son . . ." Ellen checked her notes again. ". . . John. He's the boy who was paralyzed from the waist down playing football last year. His mother said that yesterday morning she felt something calling to her to look out her bedroom window, and there was the Virgin. She made the workers stop digging right away."

Donna, the most timid woman who had ever worked for him, raised her hand, which he had made clear was never necessary in his newsroom. He nodded her way. "How does Mrs. Nichols know it's really the Virgin?" she said in a voice so low everyone had to lean toward her to hear.

"Because," Ellen said, "she's been praying to her for help every day since her son's accident."

"Q.E.D.," Simon said, and Ellen laughed a little, his audience of one. "Seems we're the only skeptics in this bunch."

Donna raised her hand again and began talking even before he acknowledged her, a big step forward, he thought. "I wrote the story when Johnny got hurt," she said. "The way his spine was crushed, the doctors didn't give him a chance. It *was* a miracle he survived."

"A medical miracle," Simon said. "But the question is how we treat this supposed appearance of the Virgin Mary now on Larkspur. Do we run a straight story, or do we hint that the whole thing's a ploy to arouse sympathy and donations?" The young reporters exchanged glances.

"Maybe it's neither," Ellen said. "Maybe Mrs. Nichols is just seeing what she wants to see."

"Can I ask something?" They all turned toward David Rigero, standing against the back wall, his foot on a chair. "I know I'm not a writer or anything, but I was wondering something."

"Shoot," Simon said.

Rigero fixed Ellen with his eyes in a way that made her look away. "Is anyone showing up there, like from the local parish?"

"Dozens of people," she said. "Whole families."

"So why are people around here looking for miracles in dirt?"

Simon wrote *Red Paint Looking for Miracles* on the easel. "That's a good angle. Talk to the people making the pilgrimage to the house, Ellen, find out why they're going there. And take David with you."

He decided to see for himself. Miracles, even imagined ones, didn't happen very often in Red Paint. He headed for the western side of town by the Bay Loop, the longer route that dipped and curved so much that even drivers familiar with the road kept two hands on the wheel. Off the right-hand side was Red Paint Bay, sparkling blue-green in the late afternoon sun. As a boy it seemed to him like the ocean itself, as big as it was, six miles around.

At the end of the loop he veered onto Larkspur. The street ahead of him was so full of parked cars that he had to pull over a block away. When he reached the sprawling Colonial at number 33 the miracle seekers were lined up on the narrow gravel path next to the house. Yellow police tape stretched across the front walk. A sign tacked to a tree pointed around back. Several women in line fingered rosaries. He heard whispers of "Hail Mary, full of grace . . ." After a few minutes shuffling forward he turned the corner into the freshly mowed backyard. There was the dirt, piled ten feet high, with a white canopy arching over it and clear plastic draping the sides. The sign staked into the ground said DONATED BY DEVEREAUX CATERERS. A computer-size cardboard box marked BLESSINGS FOR THE VIRGIN sat next to the mound. The woman in front of him pulled out a twenty-dollar bill from her pocket and dropped it in, then crossed herself and kissed her fingers. A man in a business suit did the same. Simon leaned over the box, saw dozens of tens and twenties. These were not spare-change miracle seekers.

"Keep moving, please," Mrs. Nichols said from her post next to the mound, coaxing people along. She was somewhat grayer than when he interviewed her after her son's accident, and thicker in the waist. Still impressive, though, almost six feet two, with no hint of stooping over. She was apparently quite comfortable with her size. The dirt did look like a face, he had to admit, and more so of a woman than a man, though he couldn't say why. There was a small rock for a nose and two slight indentations where eyes would be. But if this was the Virgin Mary, she didn't have ears, hair, or much of a chin, as far as he could make out.

Mrs. Nichols touched his shoulder. "Please step back if you want to linger." Simon started to move on, but she grabbed his arm. "Mr. Howe," she said, "I didn't recognize you."

"Nice to see you again, Mrs. Nichols. How's John?"

She tipped her head to the upstairs window, and there was the boy staring out at the scene in the yard. A round red face and shaved head. "He's doing fine now. He feels his whole life has been blessed."

Simon found himself nodding, but to what—a miraculous blessing of this yard, this house, this paralyzed boy? A woman pressed against his side and gave him a little shove. "Quite a crowd you're getting," he said as he stepped out of her way.

"Channel 13's coming out tonight from Portland. They said CBS may pick up the feed, go national. We'll be mobbed, but I couldn't keep this to myself and Johnny. That wouldn't be right." She let go of his arm. "Sorry I couldn't give the *Register* an exclusive, though. I did call you first."

"I understand," Simon said.

Mrs. Nichols closed her eyes. "Can't you feel it?"

"It?"

"The spirit of Our Lady."

Simon looked back at the pyramid of brown earth, and now the Virgin seemed to be smiling at him.

Four

Fox Run was silent. Standing at the edge of his yard with the mail in his hands, Simon listened. Where were the speeding cars, the mothers calling back wandering children, or the rude teens skateboarding treacherously down the sidewalk? Where were the backfires that sounded like gunshots, or the gunshots that sounded like backfires? Where were the foxes running? The street was uncommonly still, even for Red Paint. He walked the slate path toward his house with the magical mound of earth in his mind. He scanned the rows of white pines on either side of the yard, his eyes searching out an unexpected pattern, some suggestion of design imprinted on nature. What he saw were the ragged branches of trees in desperate need of pruning.

He opened the front door and shouted hello, as he always did, extending the word into nonsense for Davey's benefit . . . "Hel-looooo."

The boy came running from the kitchen, an Oreo clenched between his lips. His sneakers were untied and his T-shirt ripped at the neck. He skidded to a stop and spit the cookie into his hand. "Anything for me, Dad?" His face contorted into an assortment of squints and stretches, as if he were auditioning to be a clown.

"No, and keep doing that, your face might stay twisted up one day, which you won't like much when you start up with girls."

"I already got a girl." Davey sucked on the Oreo.

"When did this happen?"

"Sometime."

"What's her name?"

Davey bit his lip, his top teeth grinding down in a sawing motion. It was a habit he had only recently started. "You're not going to call her parents or anything."

"I just want to know who you're hanging out with."

Davey ran his fingers through his hair, propping it higher. "It's Tina." He turned to go before any more questions could be asked of him.

"Hey," Simon said, "you didn't mow the lawn again today."

"I know," the boy answered wearily, as if he was always confirming the obvious to his father. "I was busy making things disappear."

"You mean making things *appear* to disappear."

Davey pulled a blue bandanna from his pocket. "Yeah, like coins and eggs. I was trying to make Casper disappear, but she won't stay still long enough." Davey opened his right hand to reveal a quarter. He draped it with the bandanna, then yanked it away. The palm was empty. "Cool, huh?" He hurried down the hallway past Amy, who patted him on the way by. She was always touching him when he came within her range. Should he do that, too, Simon wondered, or was it more of a mother's thing?

She nodded at the mail in his hands. "Anything besides bills?"

He shook his head. "Sometimes I think we're raising a very odd boy."

She glanced behind herself, but Davey was already gone. "He seems normal enough to me."

"You don't think it's strange for him to sit inside all afternoon trying to make things disappear?"

"You're the one who bought him the magic book."

Simon set the mail down on the hall table, and as he did his fingers felt the slickness of a postcard on the bottom. He pulled it out and saw a giant Ferris wheel with the inscription, THE COLUMBIAN EXPOSITION, CHICAGO, 1893. He read the message out loud: "Greetings from the City of Big Shoulders. I saw one of those adages today that everybody is supposed to believe. It said: Expect the worst and you won't be disappointed. Faithfully . . ."

Amy touched his arm. "This is getting weird, Simon."

He read the message again. "It's just a little philosophizing."

"It doesn't bother you getting strange notes in the mail?"

"I figure the sender's just confused me with somebody else."

"How many Simon Howes do you think there are in Maine?"

"Apparently at least one other."

She headed for the kitchen, and he followed her. "So," he said as she took a sponge and wiped the counter, "aren't you going to ask what I'm leading with this week?"

"What are you leading with this week, Simon?"

"The Virgin Mary."

"She's back?"

"Yep. In a yard on Larkspur, ensconced in a mound of dirt."

Amy took out pots of various sizes from the cabinet drawers, banging them as she did. She wasn't a delicate cook, but she was quick. "Does this dirt look any more like her than the freezer frost?"

"I'd say it resembles a face like the Man on the Moon does. If you want to see the Virgin Mary, you can." Amy opened the refrigerator and searched through the crowded shelves until she found the containers she was looking for. She left the door slightly open, a habit of hers, and Simon nudged it shut with his foot. "You'd think people would expect more from their miracles," he said, "not just someone sitting in dirt."

"Are you going to run a story?"

"We have to. The line of people is already stretching out to the street."

"Why don't you get Father Elliott to say it's a hoax? You know he finds this stuff embarrassing."

Simon pulled out a stool from under the counter and sat partway on it. "I went through this the last time with him. Privately he'll tell me it's bullshit, but for attribution all he'll say is that the Church has a rigorous process for determining miracles, and he's pleased with the demonstration of faith by so many people."

Amy lined up stalks of celery on the cutting board, then chopped them quickly into one-inch sections. It amazed him how close she was willing to come to her fingers. "It's blind faith," she said as she brushed the celery into a pan.

"What faith isn't blind?" Simon leaned down to rub Casper's back as she ate. The cat whipped her head around, a warning, and Simon withdrew his hand. "Maybe I'll dub her *Our Lady of Red Paint* in a 60-point headline over a picture. That would put us on the map. I could spark a whole new industry selling Red Paint dirt. The Chamber of Commerce would love it."

"What happens when it rains?"

"They have her covered with a canopy. And I'm sure they'll recarve her features every night. The Virgin will be staying in town with us for a while, if Mrs. Nichols has anything to say about it. She won't let go easily."

Amy dumped a container of leftover white rice onto a plate, and it clumped in the center, box-shaped. She flattened it with a wooden spoon. "And you said nothing ever happens in Red Paint."

Five

The thought of being feted by the Red Paint Area Rotary Club of America left Simon feeling vaguely depressed. Was this the pinnacle of his achievements as a journalist, the most he could hope for? He was the editor of a weekly newspaper in a town known only for the ancient Indian inhabitants who left huge shell heaps in the sand, remnants of their great feasts, and painted their dead with ocher. A thousand years later he was sitting on a raised platform in the Bayswater Inn watching fifty Rotarians jab their forks into Boston cream pie. And he had to listen to himself being praised in a way that seemed perilously close to eulogy.

"A decade ago the *Register* was going bankrupt," Rotary president Jim Concannon continued. "Red

Paint was in danger of losing its voice. Simon Howe gave up a promising career as a reporter in Portland to return to his roots after his folks died. We all know he used his inheritance to buy the paper and pay off its debts. It's not a glamorous job, editor of a small-town weekly. I'm sure we've all called over complaining to Simon about something he didn't print or did print."

There was a little laughter from around the room, and Simon smiled as if *no hard feelings.*

"Today," Concannon said, "we recognize Simon Greenleaf Howe with our Medal of Community Service."

Simon jumped up quickly and whispered, "Thanks for the kind words" in the president's ear. He only had to wait a moment for the clapping to die down. He surveyed the dozen tables, each with four or five local business people. He knew almost all of them by name or face, even the ones he hadn't actually met.

"I started out at the *Register* as a delivery boy when I was ten," he began. "I probably tossed papers under the cars of a few of you." Simon sipped from his water glass, allowing a moment for the gentle laughter. "President Concannon suggested I recall some of the most memorable stories we've run over the years. I remember this headline vividly—*High School Dropouts Cut in Half.* Seems a bit Draconian to me. Then there was *Police Suspect Foul Play in Murder.* Can't put much over on Red Paint's finest." Chief Garrity smiled and waved from the back table when everyone looked his way. "We haven't spared the school committee with our precision headlines, either. A few years ago we reported on page one, *Initiative Seeks to Wipe Out Literacy*."

The Rotarians were wildly laughing now, as he expected. People always enjoyed hearing the errors of others. "To be honest," he said, "I didn't know what I was doing when I bought the *Register*. I learned fast that the paper is not just a chronicle of individual lives—the birth announcements and school sports, the marriages and promotions, the fire and police logs, and finally, the obituaries. A good paper is a portrait of the town itself. Sometimes the picture isn't what we'd like to present or what you want to read—teenagers knocking over the gravestones in the Veterans Cemetery, for example, or the brawl at the hockey game last year. But there's far more good in the picture—far more good in Red Paint—and we make sure you see that. It's not the whole story. Much of life goes on inside families and churches and offices and stores—out of sight of our photographer and reporters. That's as it should be. The *Register* strives to reflect the public life of the town with honesty and accuracy—the same goal as every community newspaper in America."

Simon stepped back from the dais. He hadn't realized how short his speech was until this moment, as the Rotarians sat there staring at him, expecting more.

It took a moment for Concannon to get up from his seat and start the applause.

Amy was in the hallway when he opened the front door, waving an oversized postcard in the air. "Your anonymous correspondent strikes again."

Simon set down his briefcase in the hallway and loosened his tie. He gave her a hug and inhaled a wonderful citrus scent, possibly grapefruit. He could never remember the name to buy it for her.

"This one's of the Liberty Bell," she said. "He's getting closer."

"It's just been three cities—Salt Lake, Chicago, and now Philadelphia. That doesn't necessarily make a pattern."

"Sure it does. Any two things are meaningless. Three show a pattern."

"Okay, what's the message this time?"

She read it dramatically, as if reciting lines in a play: "I learned a valuable lesson from you some time ago. I am now in a position to pay you back. Come to the River View Restaurant in Bath, Sat. July 2, 7 p.m. Faithfully . . ."

"So maybe these cards have a point after all," Simon said as he took off his jacket.

"Which is?"

"That I helped someone in my generous past, and that person wants to repay me with dinner. The mystery will be solved July 2 at seven p.m."

Amy inspected the message more closely. "It's written ambiguously. *Pay you back* could mean getting even."

"Why would you jump to that idea?"

"You're a journalist. The stories you run in the *Register* aren't always positive. Like that sex registry last month. There were a lot of mistakes you had to correct the next issue."

"There were two mistakes in the level of offense, and they weren't our fault. The state gave us incorrect information."

"Still, somebody on that list could hold you responsible for ruining their reputation. They might want to get back at you somehow."

"And you think they'd go to this elaborate effort, starting out in Salt Lake City and letting me know they're coming?"

"Revenge is often elaborate. That's part of its appeal. You get to enjoy it over and over again as you plan it."

He searched for a hanger in the hall closet but couldn't find one. He wanted to ask why there never were enough hangers, but that would imply that she was in charge of them. He slipped his jacket around another one and turned back into the hall. "When did you become an expert on revenge?"

She handed him the postcard. "I'm an expert on people, and I don't think you should meet this person."

"Nothing's going to happen at the River View."

"It has those huge windows. Somebody could take a shot at you from outside."

The thought of being a target amused Simon. Had he somehow fallen into a cliché mystery novel? "I won't sit by the windows or on the deck out back, how's that?"

"I'm serious, Simon. You don't know who this guy is or what he intends."

"This person has become a *he* in your opinion?"

She pointed at the writing. "Look how large the letters are and the way the words crowd in at the end of the line. No woman writes like that."

"Messiness is a male trait?"

"On postcards it is."

"All right, I admit there's a small risk responding to an anonymous note. But it might make a good human interest story for the paper. I'm going to meet *him*."

"Then I'll go with you."

"You weren't invited."

"Nevertheless, I'm going."

It was useless to try to persuade her otherwise, so Simon just nodded and headed for the stairs. "How did your speech go?" she called after him.

"I was triumphant," he said as he mounted the steps. "A standing ovation, if you count the busboys waiting at the back for me to finish so they could clear the tables. They were standing at least."

"I'm sure you knocked 'em dead."

Davey was late for dinner, which wasn't like him. He always turned up on time for food. "Maybe he's kicking his soccer ball around out back," Amy said as she set the dining room table.

Simon opened the side door to check the yard as a black-and-white Red Paint police cruiser pulled into the driveway. The possibilities raced through his mind—Davey struck by a car, Davey caught shoplifting, Davey smoking or drinking. Simon ran to the squad car and saw his son sitting in the backseat, his arms folded in his lap, staring straight ahead with a fierce expression on his face, like a criminal who doesn't believe he should be treated as a criminal.

Officer Jim Daly, the oldest patrolman on the force, hoisted himself out of the driver's side. "Everything's all right, Simon. Just a little scrap on the Common your kid got into, so I thought I'd bring him home to you."

Daly opened the back door and Davey slid out, his head down. Simon squatted so that he was eye level with his son. There weren't any visible bumps or bruises. His clothes weren't torn. He didn't look like he'd been in a fight at all, which made Simon feel a little proud. Apparently he had gotten the best of it. "You okay?"

"Yeah."

Yes, Simon thought, say *yes* for once in your life. "What happened?" Davey kicked at the gravel in the driveway. Simon looked up at the officer.

"Why don't you send him inside and we can talk?"

"Go in and wash up for dinner, Davey. You're late, and you had Mom worried."

"It's nothing serious," Daly said as the youngster trudged across the lawn. "I was driving by the bandstand and saw a scuffle going on. I separated the kids and thought it best if I brought Davey home."

"Is the other boy okay?"

Daly rubbed his hands over his face. "Actually, it was a girl."

"A girl?"

"Tina Squires. She's a pretty big girl, I'll say that. She could have hurt him if she'd landed a punch."

Simon tried to picture the scene. "You're telling me my son was fighting with a girl?"

The policeman nodded. "Seems she called him a little shrimp."

That was, Simon figured, the worst insult that could be hurled at the second-smallest boy in his class. And not just from a girl, but from Tina, his girlfriend.

"Kids can be cruel," Daly said, "that hasn't changed since I grew up. Still . . ."

"Yes," Simon said, "still."

Six

Simon stared at the rack of summer shirts in his closet. He reached for a green-striped one, which he often wore to the office, then slipped it back on the hanger. He pulled out a blue linen, his going-out-to-dinner-with-Amy shirt, and held it up. "Is this dressy enough or too dressy?"

She leaned on his shoulder to steady herself putting on a shoe. "It's dinner at the River View in Bath. A sweatsuit is too dressy."

He returned the blue linen and took out a basic black cotton shirt. "This guy might be bringing a camera to capture the moment when he hands me a thousand-dollar check for something I did for him. I'd like to look sharp for that."

He put on the shirt, and she licked her finger and rubbed at a spot on the front. "I still wish you'd change your mind."

"If someone was planning to shoot at me, they wouldn't have to lure me to Bath to do it. They could drive down Mechanic Street and fire away at me through the window."

"That makes me feel better."

He pulled her toward him and felt the whole shape of her pressed against him. He loved her firmness, nothing frail or brittle about her. She wouldn't break easily, but she did worry. "I really don't need a body-guard," he said.

"If you go, I go."

Simon picked up the car keys from the hall table and called upstairs, "We're leaving, Davey."

The boy jumped out at the top of the steps as if hiding there. "See ya," he said, then pushed in his earbuds. Amy motioned for him to pull them out.

"Check the back door for Casper in a little while and feed her the soft food when she comes in."

"Okay, Mom."

"And remember, you're grounded."

"I remember."

"We're going to the River View Restaurant up in Bath. I left my cell number on the kitchen table if you need us."

"I know your cell, Mom."

"If you have any problem, just go next door to the Benedettis'. They're always home."

"I thought I was grounded."

"If there's an emergency, we'll suspend that so you can go over there. I put some chicken nuggets in the microwave for you. Just heat them for two minutes."

"Okay."

"And don't forget . . ."

Simon took her arm. "You almost done with the reminders?"

"Almost." She looked upstairs to give her last instruction, but Davey was gone.

On the long, winding road to Bath, Simon imagined the moment opening the door to the River View. All eyes would turn toward him, everyone let in on the surprise. He would survey the crowd, face to face, until one would stand out. He'd point and laugh— *"You? You've got to be kidding me."* Then it would all come back to him, the gesture he had made that seemed so small at the time but became a life-changing act.

Amy fished in her pocketbook and pulled out lipstick. "You think we were too hard on Davey?"

"Too hard? He hit a girl on the Common. A *girl*."

Amy applied the lipstick. "He says he only shoved her, and he was provoked."

"He still can't be shoving girls around."

"Shoving boys is okay?"

"In some circumstances, yes, I'd say shoving boys is an appropriate response to a provocation."

"I assume you didn't tell him that."

"I told him he shouldn't hit or shove anyone. I don't know what's gotten into him. He's tearing around the house punching and kicking the air all the time."

"Summer," Amy said, "that's what got into him."

"We should have sent him to camp again. He said he wanted to stay home to make money cutting lawns, but he's only done the Benedettis'. He just hangs around all day trying to make Casper disappear."

"At least he hasn't succeeded," Amy said. "Be thankful for that."

The River View Restaurant once lived up to its name, with the Kennebec flowing past its back windows, just fifty yards away. Now the view was of the red brick Riverside Luxury Condominiums, squeezed kitty-cornered into the once open space. They sat at a small table for two, one aisle back from the window, and sipped Molson ales. Whenever a man entered they looked at each other and shook their heads. Too passive, too cheerful, too unimaginative. Definitely not the revenge type.

Amy reached over and took his hands. "Even if no-body shows up, it's nice to get out by ourselves."

Simon surveyed either side of the River View—the steamy kitchen to the right behind a small parti-tion, with the cooks chattering in some indecipherable tongue, and the pea green wall to the left, spotted with large fish photos. "I would have chosen someplace a bit more romantic for us than this."

A young waitress came by with her notepad poised in her hand. "Still waiting for your third?"

Amy checked her watch. "It's 7:40. We shouldn't sit here any longer without eating, Simon. People are waiting for tables."

"People waiting at the River View—that defies logic," he said, then remembered the waitress. "I just meant it's surprising your being so crowded on a Thursday night."

"We're crowded every night. Are you ready to order then?"

"I'll have the meatloaf special," Amy said.

"Very good. And you, sir?"

Simon scratched his head at her choice. "Meatloaf?"

"When in Rome."

"Right, okay, make it two, I guess."

"You're disappointed," Amy said as the waitress left.

"I just thought this might be something fun for a change. But here we're sitting in the worst restau-rant within fifty miles of Red Paint getting ready to eat a loaf of meat. That's a pretty good joke somebody played on me."

Amy looked around. "If it's a joke, the person must be here watching. Otherwise how would he enjoy it?"

"Good point."

They scanned the seats over each other's shoulders.

"We can rule out all the families and couples, it's probably a single guy." Amy nodded behind him, toward the bar. "Don't look now, but how about the man behind you with the bag on his lap? Maybe he's got your thousand bucks reward in there in small bills."

Simon glanced over as if looking at the wall clock. "No," he said, turning back, "too . . ."

"Wait," Amy said, "here he comes."

The man walked up to their table, clutching a leather messenger bag to his chest, and nodded at Amy. "I couldn't help noticing you were looking at me. Have we met before?"

"I don't think so," she said, "but it's funny, because I thought you were looking at us, and I was wondering the same thing—whether we had met before."

"I'm sure we haven't." The man tipped his head and left.

"I still think that could be him," Amy said as she leaned into the aisle to see the man push through the exit door. "Maybe we should follow him, get his license plate."

"And do what?"

"You could get your contact at motor vehicles to run the number."

Simon drank the last of his water. "If that's the mysterious card sender, he's had his fun."

Seven

He sits motionless in a maroon Chevy Lumina, the most nondescript of automobiles. The *Register* lies folded across his lap. As each man walks toward the River View, he glances down at the thumbnail photo accompanying the editor's column, *Setting the Record Straight.* Shortly after seven o'clock a white Toyota pulls into the parking lot and turns into a space a few cars down. The driver steps out, tries to glimpse the river through the buildings. The waiting man doesn't have to check the picture. Even from a distance he can tell. His face flushes, his pulse races. Can he do this? Do what exactly? He's only planned so far ahead, to this moment outside an unremarkable restaurant, sitting in a forgettable rental car waiting for his invited guest to appear. *What am I going to do now, God? Do You know?*

A car door slams shut. Then a second one. He leans forward and sees a slim dark-haired woman walking next to Simon Howe. They stroll past the Lumina oblivious to the possibility that anyone might be sitting inside there, watching them. How can people be so unaware of the threat around them? She whispers something in his ear and they clasp hands, like school kids at a dance. In a few seconds they are at the restaurant entrance. They go inside and stand by the large window, talking to the hostess. The man in the car raises his right hand, his index finger sighting the target, his thumb cocked. How easy it would be to kill someone. Motivation is never the problem, nor opportunity. Only will.

He didn't expect this, facing two of them. It throws him off. He assumed he would reach this point and find Providence taking his arm, steering him down one course or another. He closes his eyes and rubs the side of his head in circular movements. He empties his mind, letting his thoughts dissolve into nothingness, and waits for the still small voice to whisper in his ear.

In a minute his hand turns the ignition key. The Lumina rumbles to life.

The house on Fox Run is smaller than he expected, just average size for Red Paint, with scrubs of bushes in the front and thick overgrown grass. It's a place that doesn't seem tended to. He would care for it if it were his, mow the lawn, thin the ungainly plants, paint the peeling shingles. People don't deserve what they aren't willing to tend to. He gets out of the car, gazes up and down the street bathed in the hazy yellow lamp light. It seems strange to him, how everything looks like something else at dusk. The hemlock in the neighboring yard like a giant hooded monk waiting to cross a courtyard at vespers. A rounded bush like the top of a head, with shaggy hair. At this time of night, you can never be sure what you're seeing. Music floats through the air, from a radio or TV, and every few seconds a dog barks, as if demanding to be let out. There could be a dog inside this house, some large mutt trained to attack anyone unfamiliar. The possibility doesn't discourage him from crossing the street and walking up the uneven slate pathway. A dog is just one more thing to watch out for.

The front door is painted sea blue, a calming color. He takes a deep breath and turns the knob. It moves a little, gives him hope, then stops. People never locked their doors in this town when he grew up there. What was the danger now? *I am. I'm the unpredictable thing people lock their doors against.* Light beams pass over him, and he turns as a police cruiser creeps past. He can't see the officers inside but waves in case they are watching. A person waving would never be considered suspicious. It wouldn't matter anyway if they stop to question him. "Just visiting an old schoolmate," he'd say. "Doesn't seem like he's home." All perfectly true, or true enough. The cruiser turns the corner and is gone.

He looks over at the neighboring house, lit up in the second floor. He considers going down the side walkway, checking the bulkhead or kitchen door, perhaps find an open window. But this early in the night he might be seen by the neighbors, and how could he explain what he is doing? A door opens at the back of the house, a screen bangs. He listens for a minute in the darkening air, trying to understand what the sounds mean. He takes a few steps and peeks around the edge of the house. In the backyard something short and quick rushes across the dark grass.

Eight

"*We're home,*" *Simon called out* as he stepped into the hallway. "Davey?"

Amy set her pocketbook on the small table. "He probably has his earphones in."

Simon watched as she glided up the stairs. He liked how easily she moved through the world, with so little apparent effort. She went out of view for a moment, then reappeared at the railing. "He's not up here."

"Check our room. He might be watching our TV."

"I already looked," she said, coming down the stairs. "Maybe he's in the cellar." She hurried by him and pulled the door open. "Davey, are you down there?"

"He wouldn't be in the cellar with the light off," Simon said. "He's scared of the dark."

She flicked on the switch and went a few steps down. "Davey?"

They listened for his answer, but Simon figured they should be listening for something else, a moan or scratching, any odd sound at all. Amy came back up and shut the cellar door behind her. Simon tried to remain casual. "He probably went for a walk."

"Davey?"

"Maybe a bike ride."

"It's dark and his bike's in the yard. I saw it when we came in."

Simon ducked to see out the side window to the house next door. The lights were on upstairs, a comforting sight, as always. "Maybe he got spooked by some noise and went over to the Benedettis' like we told him. I'll give them a call." Simon picked up the hall phone and dialed, trying not to rush. She was watching. "Hey Bob, this is Simon next door. David's not over at your place, is he?" Simon shook his head so that Amy could see the answer. "No, nothing's wrong. We just got back after being out, and he isn't here. We thought he might have gotten a little scared and gone to your place. But he's probably just down the street at a friend's."

Simon hung up the phone. "All right," he said, "let's go over the possibilities." She just stared at him, waiting. It was obviously his responsibility to come up with a plausible reason why their grounded son would not be home. "I guess he could be out looking for Casper."

"She's sleeping on Davey's bed," Amy said.

"Maybe a friend called him to come over."

"He'd leave a note if he went out. I've told him to do that a thousand times." She hurried to the kitchen, with Simon following. Her eyes swept across the counters for a scrap of paper.

"He's not going to leave a note telling us he's doing something he shouldn't," Simon said. "He probably thought he'd be back before we got home. We told him not to expect us before 9:30."

She looked past him to the phone on the wall. "Check the call list."

He picked up the receiver and punched the directory button. "There's one at 8:15—Unknown Caller."

She grabbed the phone from him and saw for herself. "Oh God." She took a step toward the hall then turned around. "I knew this was too soon to start leaving him alone."

"Girls are babysitting at his age, Amy."

"He's not a girl. He's an immature boy," she said, her voice rising. He reached toward her with a calming hand, but she jerked backward. "You just couldn't resist the idea that someone was going to hand you a million dollars for doing something wonderful."

A thousand dollars, Simon thought. "Look, this isn't about me. It's—"

"Of course it's about you—*Master* Simon Howe."

"Nobody could know we'd leave Davey alone. You could have been home, or we could have dropped him off at a friend's, or—"

She slapped the counter with her hand. "Would you shut up and call the police?"

Simon couldn't remember Amy ever speaking to him like this. But Davey was missing, so he did shut up and dial 911.

Of the ten men on the Red Paint police force, he knew nine. The tenth, a new patrolman barely out of training, stood in the Howe living room rocking from one leg to the other. "Which restaurant did you say it was, Mr. Howe?"

"The River View, in Bath," Simon repeated, resisting the urge to suggest that Officer Reade write the name down this time.

"Is your boy used to you leaving him alone?"

"He's eleven," Simon said, "and this is his second time home alone at night."

"If he knew you were going all the way to Bath, he might have went downtown to hang out for a while. A lot of kids skateboard in the Common in the summer."

"Our son wouldn't do that."

"How can you be sure?"

"Because he was grounded."

"I see," the young policeman said, and Simon wondered what exactly he saw. "Bath's pretty far away. Do you go to the River View regularly?"

"No, the food's lousy."

"Think so? I used to live up that way. Went there all the time."

"I guess it appeals to different tastes."

Amy jumped up from her chair between them. "Would you two stop debating the stupid food? Davey's missing."

Reade rolled his eyes at Simon as if *Can't you control your wife?* The truth was, no, he couldn't. He said, "I know you're upset, Amy, but—"

"Don't be condescending."

"I'm sure Officer Reade is just following the protocol for getting the information he needs."

"Then speed up the damn protocol."

"How did you come to go to the River View," Reade said with what seemed to Simon like intentional slowness, "if you think the food's so bad?"

"I suppose you could say we were invited."

"Invited by who?"

"We don't know by whom. I received a postcard last week from someone saying he wanted to repay me for something I did."

"Can I see this postcard?"

Simon gestured to Amy. She rooted through her pocketbook, her hand plunging in and out of the various pockets. "Just dump everything out," he said.

"It's not here. We must have left it on the table at the restaurant."

"You left it at the restaurant?"

"*We* left it."

"But that's our only connection to—wait a minute, I kept the other ones."

Simon hurried to the kitchen. The yellow fish magnet was gone from the side of the refrigerator. So were the postcards. He came back to the living room empty-handed. "They aren't there."

Reade nodded as if that confirmed some theory of his. "How were you and your son getting along, Mr. Howe?"

"Why are you asking that?"

The policeman shrugged as if the reason was obvious. "You said he was grounded. Did he get into trouble recently?"

"Is that important?"

"It might figure into where he is, if we knew what was bothering him."

"Okay, what he did was swing his fist at a classmate."

"Your son hit him?"

"It was more of a shove," Simon said, "but he shouldn't be touching anybody like that. That's why we grounded him for a week."

"Did you do anything else—corporal punishment of any sort?"

"I don't think the best way to teach our son that hitting someone's bad is by hitting him ourselves."

Reade shrugged. "There's a lot of that happening these days, more than you'd think. My parents hit us big time."

Simon imagined the page-one story—*Spanking Makes a Comeback in Red Paint.* Another scarier headline popped into his mind—*Search on for Editor's Son.*

"I'm a therapist," Amy said with her fingers touching at the tips, her way of keeping composed, "and I would never spank a child. So before I explode would you get on your radio and broadcast that our son is missing?"

Reade nodded amiably, as if he was agreeing with her. But then, "The thing is, we don't really know he's missing, Mrs. Howe. All we know is that he isn't where you expected him to be. Happens all the time with kids." The officer walked to the front door and crouched down to inspect the knob. "No sign of forced entry here or at any of the windows. It appears your son let himself out. Maybe a friend rang the bell and he answered it."

"He knows not to open the door when we're not here," Simon said.

"Your boy always do what you tell him?"

"No, but—"

"I'll alert night patrol to check around town, the usual places kids hang out. You have a recent picture of . . ."

"Davey," Amy said, "our son's name is Davey." She pointed to the mantel, and Simon understood that he was to retrieve the photo of their son in his baseball uniform.

"Cute kid," the policeman said as he tucked the picture inside his jacket.

Simon nodded. Davey was a very cute kid.

Amy slammed the door shut behind the officer. "We wasted an hour with that idiot," she said. "You know how far someone can drive in an hour?"

"Drive?"

"Yes, drive. If that lunatic of yours knocked on the door and Davey answered . . ."

Simon took her hands. "I'm sure that didn't happen, Amy."

She broke away from him. "How can you say that? You don't know."

"I just think we should stay positive. We don't need both of us going to pieces."

She whirled around, her hand swiping over the hall table, sending a pile of envelopes to the floor. "Maybe that's exactly what we need, both of us feeling the same thing. Because right now I have no idea what you're feeling. It's like you know something about this."

Simon bent down to pick up the mail and set it back on the table. It took him a moment to realize what she was suggesting. "You think I'd hide information when Davey's missing?"

"I'm checking his room again," she said and then swept up the stairs faster than he had ever seen. He had to take the steps by two to keep up. She stopped just outside the doorway to Davey's room, as if not to disturb a crime scene. "Nothing's out of place," she said, which was easy to tell. Davey kept an unusually tidy room. Casper raised her head, stretched, then jumped off the bed and trotted to them. Amy picked her up and sniffed, as if there might be some clue.

Simon looked around the room for clues, anything not right, and spotted Davey's blue bandanna hanging over the bureau mirror. "This better not be one of his magic tricks or I'm going to—"

There was a sound downstairs, a door opening. The cellar door? Casper kicked out of Amy's hands, claws bared, and darted under the bed, a blur of white. She wasn't often spooked like this.

"Davey?" Amy called. There was no answer. Simon took a step, and Amy grabbed his arm. "Take his bat."

He reached around the doorway into the bedroom and pulled out the Louisville Slugger. He moved quietly down the stairs, with Amy just behind him. At the bottom he turned and looked toward the kitchen. There was their son, earphones in, pulling apart an Oreo.

"Davey!" Simon yelled and ran into the kitchen. He took the boy by the shoulders. "Are you okay?" The cookie fell to the floor.

"God, Dad, what are you doing?" Davey bent down to retrieve the Oreo.

"Where were you? We told you you were grounded."

The boy pulled out his earphones. "What?"

Amy turned her son around, her hands on his shoulders, her face level to his. "Where were you?"

"Up in the tree house. You didn't say I had to stay *in* the house. Grounded means staying in your house *or* yard."

"I'm not interested in technicalities," Simon said, turning the boy back to him. "When we leave you in the house we expect to find you in the house."

Davey started to lick the icing off the Oreo, but Amy took it from him and tossed it in the sink. "Listen to us," she said. "We've been home an hour worried sick about where you were."

"Wow," the boy said, "and you called the police?"

"You mean you saw the police car and still didn't come in?"

"I just saw it leaving like a minute ago, Mom. I didn't know it was about me." Davey reached into the cookie jar and brought out another Oreo. "Can I have this one?" Amy nodded. He twisted apart the cookie and handed the icingless side to her. "Did they catch him?"

"Catch who?" Simon asked.

"The man out front. That's why I went up the tree house. You told me not to answer the door."

"Somebody rang the doorbell?"

"He didn't ring it, but he was standing there for like a long time." Davey pointed down the hallway to the panel of fluted glass next to the front door. "So I sneaked out the back and climbed the tree and pulled up the ladder and listened to some tunes. That was the right thing to do, wasn't it?"

It was horrible to imagine, a man at the front door, not ringing the bell, just waiting, with their son inside alone. "Yes," Simon said, "that was the right thing to do."

Nine

The streets of Red Paint feel familiar to him, a pattern indelibly implanted on his brain when it was a younger age. He remembers the shortcut from the inn to the Common, parks on the darker river side, then walks the winding bike path to the bandstand. He goes up the broad steps and stops for a moment, looking out on the green as if there is a crowd come just to hear him. What would he speak of, something topical, like divine intervention in the modern world? Miracles would surely be the talk of the town after the page-one headline in the *Register—Virgin Appears in Red Paint Backyard?* The question mark was necessary, of course, the proper journalistic skepticism. But if you believe in God, how could you not believe in miracles? An all-powerful God could clearly do what would seem improbable or impossible, the definition of a miracle. He could even defy the logic that He Himself created— go up and down at the same time. Appear and disappear. Kill and let live. Punish and forgive. Be God and not be God. And He could be everywhere at once, no need to send the Virgin or anyone else as an emissary. He might even descend to a bandstand like this, in a small town like this, to deliver His message, perhaps ten new commandments for the new millennium. He would require a proper introduction, of course, and who would get the honor? *Ladies and gentleman, boys and girls, put your hands together for the Creator of* . . .

He sees something in the shadows of the bandstand floor, reaches out his foot to turn it over. A small face stares up at him, a brown teddy bear with a red strip sewn on as a smile. He picks up the spindly little stuffed animal, apparently lost or thrown away. Either way, gone from whoever once loved it. He shakes the bear of dirt and its head bounces up and back, an involuntary yes. There's no one nearby to ask about it, just youngsters kicking a soccer ball under the lamplight in the grass below. How many of these boys secretly clutch a stuffed animal to their chests at night?

He takes the teddy bear with him down the other side of the bandstand, holding the railing as he goes. He used to tear across here and leap the half-dozen steps— the single daring act of his boyhood. He remembers the terror of it, closing his eyes at takeoff, eternity in the air, his arms windmilling to keep himself aloft, then the wonderful solidness landing on earth.

The boys on the Common scramble after the soccer ball, crash into one another, then roll on the ground in exaggerated injury, clutching their calves, little fakers in training. They don't take any notice of a man strolling along with no apparent purpose. He can't remember noticing adults passing by either when he sat against the lamppost as a boy, watching the nightly Wiffle ball game his classmates organized. They coaxed him into playing once when they needed an extra kid and let him throw the ball up for himself when he batted, since he couldn't hit a regular pitch. Still, the best he could hope for was a little dribbler that he could beat out to first base, a pizza box. At least he could run fast.

He walks zigzag now across the worn-down playing field. It was always dusty here in summer, more brown than green, more dirt than grass. It hurt hitting the hard dry ground of summer.

"Hey, mister!" He looks around, sees boys behind him, boys on the side, boys in front of him. "Get out of the way, will ya?"

He waves his apology and hurries through the Common, comes to Mechanic Street and crosses without bothering to check each way. There's little traffic this time of night in Red Paint, and people would always stop for a man shuffling across the road. The

Register Building is lit up on the inside as always. He presses his face to the window and can see the old fireman's bell hanging from the ceiling, rung when the paper went to press. There's the typesetter's table in the corner, full of the cast metal letters used to make up pages by hand. And on the far wall, the old map of the Province of Maine with "Red Paint Territory" marking the land between the ocean and bay. Nothing, it appears, has changed at the *Register*.

He moves to the front door and reads the staff list posted under glass. At the top, *Simon Howe: Editor in Chief*. There are a dozen names below him, ending with *Pressroom: David Rigero*, written in a different typeface, an obvious addition. He looks both ways on the sidewalk, then takes out a Magic Marker from his pocket. He uncaps it and holds it under his nose for a moment, inhaling the pungent scent. He considers how to fit the word on the door. Angled seems best, top left to bottom right, for maximum size and dramatic effect. The marker squeaks across the surface, leaving thick black letters on the light wood color. He can't decide on the punctuation. An exclamation point? Too frantic. A period? Too formal.

He hears a car coming up the street, and it scares him that he might be seen. He can't remember ever being caught doing anything wrong, not even being reprimanded at school. He has spent so much of his life avoiding being rebuked, yet here he is defacing a building in the center of his hometown. How would he explain himself? Momentary insanity? Continuous insanity?

He sets the teddy bear against the door and slips sideways a few steps into the alley, leaving the single word to stand by itself, no punctuation needed.

Ten

RAPIST

Simon stood outside the front door to the *Register* staring at the word. Beside him, the paper's photographer raised his camera to his eye. Simon turned quickly, knocking his arm. "No pictures, Ron."

The young man regained his balance and readjusted the Nikon dangling from his neck. "Why don't you want a snap, boss? This would grab the eye on page one."

"Did anyone else see this?"

Ron turned half around as an old woman shuffled past, her head down. "Sure, I mean, anybody who goes by can see it, if they look over."

"Any staff?"

"Most of editorial is already here."

"How about the production people?"

"Nobody except Rigero. I saw his truck parked in the lot."

Simon ran his index finger over the letters, and a little of the black rubbed off.

Ron held out a battered old teddy bear. "I found this leaning against the door, like a calling card. You know, the *Teddy Bear Vandal*—good headline, huh?"

Simon took the flimsy stuffed animal. It was pressed in at the face, as if stepped on, and cut open in the belly, a small, ragged slit.

"The police will be over in a few minutes," Ron said.

Simon whirled on him. "You called the police?"

"Yeah, they always check out vandalism."

"This is just a little graffiti, probably from some bored kid. Get something abrasive from the janitor's room and we'll rub it off."

"That's bad business, that's what it is." The voice came with a wooden cane shaking between their heads. Simon and Ron leaned out of the way as Erasmus Hall jabbed it toward the door. "It's a sign," he said, "repent before it's too late." He held out a tract. Simon took one from his tremoring hand and then stood in front of the word until it could be washed away.

"Mr. Howe, can I talk to you a minute?"

Simon looked up from his desk and saw his recently hired pressroom man standing over him. He smelled of

after-shave, some strong metallic scent. "Sure." Simon
scanned the newsroom. "We could go in the conference
room, that would be private."

"I don't need private. This is okay."

Simon gestured to the seat across his desk, then
leaned over it. "The writing on the door—I guess you
saw it."

"Yeah, there was kind of a crowd out there when I
pulled in, so I took a look."

"I'm sorry," Simon said. "We scrubbed it off as soon
as I got in."

"You're sorry?"

"That you had to see it."

Rigero shrugged, his shoulders sticking up longer
than usual, like a child who hasn't quite mastered the
gesture. "Doesn't have anything to do with me. Nobody knows what I was in for except you," he said, his
voice a little lower, "and you didn't tell anybody, did
you, Mr. Howe, because that would be like invading
my privacy, wouldn't it?"

He'd told Amy, but wives didn't count. Everyone
presumed you shared secrets with your spouse. "Of
course I didn't tell anyone."

"Then nobody else would know."

Simon nodded. "So what is it you wanted to talk to
me about?"

"I was making up the For Sale page and saw your
ad for the piano."

"You play?" The question popped out of Simon with more surprise in his voice than was appropriate. "I mean, you didn't mention that when we talked about your hobbies at the interview."

"It's not for me. I got a sister up in Brunswick has three kids. I thought I'd refinish it for her, like a gift. She used to play when we were growing up. I figure she could teach her kids."

"That's a nice idea."

"She stuck by me when I was in, my sister did. The rest of the family acted like I died."

"I'm sorry to hear that. But the piano, it's been used pretty hard. My son used to play with his feet. And it hasn't been tuned in years."

"That's okay, I'm used to working with wood, and I'll get it tuned. But I was wondering, the ad said a hundred dollars, would you take seventy-five? That's all I got."

Haggling over the price of her piano—Amy wouldn't like that. He would have to say he got the full amount and chip in the other twenty-five himself. "Sure," Simon said. How could he ask for more than all a person had?

"I got my truck, I could come around after work and pick it up."

"It's pretty heavy."

Rigero flexed his arms a little. "I used to be a mover, and I have a lift on my truck. I can handle it." He stood up and put out his hand to seal the deal.

"You know," Simon said as they shook, "maybe we better go over now before my wife gets home. She isn't thrilled we're getting rid of this. She might chase you away," he said, laughing just a little.

"Okay, I'll meet you there," Rigero said and headed for the pressroom.

Simon grabbed his jacket and turned toward the front door. He had never noticed before, the self-segregation of the editorial and press staffs in their entrances and exits. Was it a pattern worth changing? "I'm off for the rest of the day," he called to Barbara across the room, and she waved at him without lifting her elbow from her desk.

The front door opened in as he reached for the handle, and Holly Green leaned up to press her cheek to his. Of all the girls in his class, Holly wore twenty-five years the best, he thought.

"I'm glad I caught you, Simon," she said, full of energy as always. "I have some stories for the reporter you assigned to the reunion story."

"Anything exciting?" he asked as he stepped back to let her in.

"I was going to tell him about our senior weekend in Boston, the last one in the history of Red Paint High."

Simon remembered the trip well—the cheap hotel on the outskirts of the city, the room hopping after curfew, the tossing of the fake Roman statues into the pool, raiding the minifridges for every available snack.

"I have to admit, we did ruin it for every other senior class."

"You can take kids out of Maine but you can't take Maine out of the kids—that's how our beloved vice-principal so condescendingly put it."

"In retrospect, I see his point," Simon said. "But go light on the details with Joe. I don't want to make us look too bad." He gave Holly a little hug to indicate he had to leave and headed off to move a piano.

"Nice place," Rigero said as he walked around the sunny family room picking up whatever could be picked up—a ceramic giraffe, a wicker basket full of old political buttons, and a round shell-like object, pocked with holes.

"Brain coral," Simon said. "Davey found it out in the front yard. This area was probably under water once."

"Or somebody just tossed it out his car window driving by."

"That's possible, too."

Rigero reached for one of the family photos lined up on the end table, then held it close to his eyes as if trying to discern some small detail.

"It's Disney World," Simon said. "We made the obligatory trip last year."

"Looks like your kid had a great time."

"Davey was in heaven."

Rigero shrugged. "Don't expect I'll get there myself."

Simon noted the careful way Rigero set the picture back on the end table at the same angle as before, as if he was familiar with the room, or at least felt at home there. A thought crossed his mind, but how could he put it? "You didn't happen to stop by here last Thursday night, did you, David?"

Rigero looked up quickly. "Why would I do that?"

"No reason," Simon said. "Our son just thought he saw someone at the front door who didn't ring the bell, and we were trying to figure out who it was."

Rigero laughed a little. "So you're asking everybody?"

"No, I mean, I just thought, since you knew where I lived maybe you stopped by for something."

Rigero squatted next to the old Endicott upright, leaned his shoulder into the side, and lifted the piano an inch off the floor. "About 250, I'd say. I've moved heavier." He held up the small throw rug he'd brought with him. "We'll shove this under it and drag it to the door."

"Sounds like a plan."

Simon heard the Volvo's sputtering motor coming up the driveway and looked out of the front window. "Christ," he said, "my wife."

"That a problem?"

"Never can tell." He hurried into the hallway and opened the door as Amy came through, humming. "You're home early," he said.

She gave him a quick kiss on the cheek. "Don't look so thrilled."

"I'm just surprised."

"My three o'clock canceled." She dropped her bag on the hall chair. "Why is a pickup in our driveway?

He gestured toward the family room and the back of the man inspecting the piano. "I found a buyer. We were going to move it before you got home, but we can do it another time."

"Don't be silly. I've made my peace with your getting rid of part of my childhood. Cart it away." She moved into the room with her arm outstretched. "I'm Amy."

Rigero turned around and shook her hand quickly, then dropped it. "Nice to meet you, I'm David."

"David," she repeated, "that's our son's name, but he insists we call him Davey."

"I've always been David."

"This will only take a few minutes," Simon said, putting his shoulder to the piano as Rigero had done. "Why don't you go get changed, Amy, while we move this out of here?"

She leaned against the arm of the sofa, not going anywhere. "How did you find a buyer so fast?"

So the questions began, leading to a predictable conclusion. "I put an ad in the paper," Simon said, "like we talked about."

Amy thought for a moment, which was what he was afraid of. "The paper doesn't come out till tomorrow."

Rigero smiled mischievously. "I guess I had an unfair advantage—I saw the ad early."

"All right," Simon said standing up now, "you do the heavy lifting, David, and I'll slip the rug under."

"You saw the ad early," Amy repeated, circling them. "You work at the *Register*?"

"Yeah, in the pressroom. Just started a couple of weeks ago." He ran his fingers smoothly over the top. "This is actually a pretty good piece. The wood's not warped at all."

"Have you tried playing it?" Amy asked.

Rigero positioned himself at the side of the piano and found two grips for his hands. "Mr. Howe told me it's out of tune—that's why he knocked twenty-five dollars off, right?"

"That I did," Simon said as he knelt down, the rug in his hand.

"You can always get a piano tuned right, but you can't fix warped wood."

"So," Amy said, her voice hardening now, "you're an expert on pianos?"

Rigero shook his head. "I just know wood."

"What else do you know?"

"Ready, lift," Simon said, and as the piano rose off the floor, he shoved the small rug under the two side legs.

Rigero set the piece gently down, then rubbed his hands together. "I guess I know a thing or two about a thing or two."

GEORGE HARRAR

Amy nodded. "Robert De Niro—*This Boy's Life.*"

"Yeah, he was great in that, wasn't he?"

"In a psychotic sort of way, yes."

Rigero grinned. "Nobody does psychotic better than De Niro."

Amy ran her hand over the top of the piano, a caress. "Prison," she said, and both men turned toward her, "is that something you know a little about?"

Rigero glanced at Simon.

"What about—"

"Amy," Simon cut in but then didn't know what to say. He had never been able to get her to hold her tongue.

She regarded him a moment, then turned back to Rigero.

"Rape?" he said. "Is that what you want to know about?"

Amy stared at him for a few moments. "Maybe Simon didn't tell you, but I'm a therapist, and my longest-running patients have been sexually assaulted."

Rigero rubbed his arm hard across his face, turning it red for a moment. "And like how many rapists do you have as clients?"

"I don't treat rapists."

"Then you only know one side of rape."

She dismissed his point with a flick of her hand. "You think there are two sides to rape?"

Rigero shrugged. "There are two sides to every-thing, if you want to listen to them."

"Okay," Simon said, stepping between them, "let's move a piano."

He helped secure the old upright in the truck, position-ing and repositioning, tying and retying. It took a half hour.

"That should hold her," Rigero said as he jumped off the back. He pulled out a pack of cigarettes from his rear pocket. The box was crushed at the top. He opened it up and tilted it toward Simon. One mangled cigarette remained inside.

A generous offer, Simon thought. "No thanks, I don't smoke."

Rigero flipped open a matchbox and pulled out the remaining match. He struck it against the light-ing strip, then cupped his hand around the flame and guided it toward the cigarette in his mouth. Such deli-cate maneuvers, the ritual of smoking. "Your wife," he said as he expelled the first long puff, "she was getting pretty hot in there."

Simon wondered at his choice of words. Not angry or upset—*hot.* "Like she said, she works with a lot of women recovering from, you know, being assaulted, so she's kind of sensitive on the subject."

"I just didn't expect it, her knowing." He said this in an offhand way, not accusatory at all.

"Sorry about that. Once she knew I hired from the prison she wouldn't let it go. She actually guessed."

Rigero dropped his half-cigarette to the street and rubbed it out with his foot. "You can tell her I was in seven to ten for having sex with a woman who passed out on me halfway through. Five minutes' pleasure, seven years' pain."

Simon couldn't imagine telling Amy this, but he nodded anyway, like one guy to another.

On his way back to the house he pulled out a few weeds growing up around the front walk. At the door he turned toward the sun and let the warm rays soak his face till it began to burn. Then he went inside.

"I can't believe it," she said, rushing into the hallway. "You brought that man into our house when I specifically warned you I never wanted to meet him."

"How could I know you'd be home early?"

"That's not the point," she said, her body visibly shaking. "A person like that is toxic, and I didn't want him anywhere near our lives. Now his disgusting hands will be playing the piano I never wanted to sell in the first place, the one I learned on and Davey learned on."

"You agreed it was taking up too much space, and it's not for him anyway. He's refinishing it for his sister who has three kids so they can have music in their lives."

"So he's a music-appreciating rapist with a heart of gold. I'm touched."

Simon shook his head at her. "Why are you getting so hysterical over this?"

"Don't use that word on me," she said. "Every time Freud wrote about an hysterical patient it was a woman."

"Okay, I take it back, you're not hysterical. But why are you so upset? He made a mistake and served his sentence."

"Because women who are raped don't get a few years' term they can serve and then they're free."

"So David deserves a life sentence? Or is that too good for him? Perhaps he should be strung up on the Common."

"Don't be sarcastic."

"I'm serious. I really want to know—what's the proper sentence for a rapist?"

Amy thought for only a moment. "Shame, Simon, and that man doesn't have any."

Eleven

He sits on the wide-planked porch of the Bayswater Inn watching rain pelt the water. At times the wind changes direction and blows the thick drops far enough sideways to reach him under the broad roof. He doesn't stir, even when the inn's owner, Peter Mc-Bride, approaches him with a mug filled with a brown liquid, topped by whipped cream.

"Compliments of the house, Mr. Chambers," the innkeeper says as he holds out the tall glass. "It's the specialty of the inn—we call it the Tonic. My grand-mother used to say if this doesn't cure what ails you, nothing ails you." The man takes the mug and paper napkin. "The secret is using Jameson whiskey and untreated Vermont cream, no chemicals. Don't stir it in. Drink through it."

He sips the sweet cream until the coffee pours through with a jolt of whiskey. He wipes his mouth on the napkin, leaving a dark smudge, which he folds out of view. "I'm not a coffee drinker," he says, "but this is very nice."

The wind whips the halyard on the flagpole, making them turn toward the curving driveway. "I could listen to that all night," McBride says. "I've always thought the best sounds on earth are a foghorn, a waterfall, and the rattle of the halyard against a flagpole."

"And the whistle of a train," the man says, "one going away from you."

McBride moves behind his guest and takes hold of a large black handle, which he turns with some effort. The blue-striped awning begins rolling up, inch by inch. "Sorry," he says, "can't chance a gust ripping through it. You might want to move inside."

"A little rain never hurt anyone," he says. But forty days and nights of it, that extinguished virtually every living thing. Six chapters after creation, God washed away humanity, repenting that He had made it. To whom does God confess?

McBride leans against an empty Adirondack chair. "I'd sit out with you if I could, but we've got a lot of work to do before the school reunion here next week.

Things get pretty chaotic for a few days. I hope you won't be put out."

"It won't bother me at all," the man says, a most agreeable guest.

He remembers the music most of all—the Adagietto from Mahler's Fifth, the strange meditation of violins and harp that always accompanied wakes at the Bayswater Inn. It seemed to him like music that didn't want to end, as if the notes were bunching up at the edge of a cliff, refusing to be shoved over. He was the body watcher at so many viewings when he was a teenager that it took years to get the haunting melody out of his head. And now it has come back as he crosses the dining room toward the Viewing Room, a small outcropping off the west wing where the bodies of Red Paint's most prominent citizens are laid out in their ornate coffins. He could have brought Jean here in her sleek bronze casket, surrounding it with large pots of white lilies. But what if no one came to her wake? What if no one remembered her at all?

He pulls open the doors and sees two computers sitting on facing desks. He steps back and looks both ways to make sure he isn't disoriented. The Viewing Room has apparently become a small media center, and where do people in Red Paint now go to say goodbye to their dead? He takes a seat at one of the monitors. The cursor blinks in the Google box, blinks and blinks, waiting for instructions.

That evening he sits in the library and prints a short message in his clearest hand, all capitals. He walks over to the reception counter where an older woman is making notes in a ledger, her head down. It's the first time he's seen her there, and he wonders what position she holds in the McBride clan. Sprawled next to her on the counter is a muscular gray cat with an enormous lionlike head.

"Oh," she says, looking up after a minute, "I didn't hear you."

It's a familiar comment—*I didn't hear you,* or *I didn't see you.* Sometimes he feels like he could walk through people and they wouldn't notice. Maybe just a little shudder and a momentary *What was that?* "Sorry to bother you," he says, "but do you have a postcard stamp, by any chance?"

"I can do better than that, I have a meter right here." She gestures behind her and then extends her hand. He holds the card down along his leg. "Anything wrong, Mr. . . ."

"Chambers."

"Of course, the Rachel Carson suite."

She's waiting for his answer. *Is anything wrong?* He hands over the postcard.

"Paul Revere," she says, noting the picture. "You should get one of our Bayswater Inn cards, show people where you're staying. Only a dollar each, I have them here."

"Perhaps next time," he says.

She slides his postcard through the meter, then tosses it into a tray of outgoing mail, message side up. At this movement the cat raises its head off the counter and considers the human close by. He has never seen a cat like this one, so thick in the neck and face.

"Have you met Terrence?" the woman asks, scratching the animal's cheek.

"Hello, Terrence."

"He looks like a bruiser, I know. The males get that way when they aren't neutered, all bulked up for fighting. But inside he's just a big sweetie." Terrence holds his gaze.

"That's nice to know." The man reaches out his index finger, and the cat takes a lick.

"If Terrence likes you," the woman says, "you must be all right."

Twelve

The postcard showed Paul Revere on the front, galloping to warn the local militias of the coming British army. The message on the back said, "You should have come alone"—an unnerving few words. Then "Faithfully yours." Amy's presence, it seemed, had indeed spooked the sender, as Simon thought it might. Apparently gone was the possibility of meeting whoever this person was and discovering what payback he intended. If Amy were there he couldn't resist showing her the card and saying *I told you not to come with me.*

She was not there, and the kitchen where he stood seemed empty without her. The house seemed empty without Davey skulking about upstairs or outside, up to something. They had gone to visit her mother

in Bangor, leaving Simon with an unusual night home
alone. He had a sudden craving for pizza, everything
on it, and ordered it delivered. He ate at the kitchen
table, drinking beer, trying to dredge up feature story
ideas.

1. Is Red Paint happy? Do a survey to com-
   pare to national stats just released.
2. Local history—why did the Red Paint People abandon their territory without a fight?
3. Question: Has Erasmus Hall persuaded
   even one person to repent? (Portrait of con-
   viction in the face of constant rejection)
4. Ongoing series—Whatever happened
   to . . . ?

The phone rang much louder than usual, and Simon
wondered if Davey had turned up the volume again,
one of his little pranks. He leaned across the table, expecting to see Amy's name on the caller ID. It was a
straight shot to Bangor on the highway, and she could
have made it in an hour, even in the light rain. The ID
said Unknown Caller.

"Hello?"

No answer, no sound at all, like a dead line, or the
few moments' delay between when the telemarketer re-
alizes his call has gone through and actually speaks. "I
don't want any," Simon said and hung up.

As he walked past his bedroom window later that night he noticed a car across the street. Every few seconds, the wipers passed across the windshield. A figure was barely visible on the driver's side, a head with a flash of white on top. The face blended into the glass, indistinguishable. Simon watched for several minutes. The car's occupant was probably pirating his neighbors' WiFi signal. Or perhaps checking a map, searching for a way out of Red Paint. Simon considered going out to help. If he weren't already undressing for bed, he was sure he would do just that.

He woke into darkness, heard a faint rubbing noise, like metal against wood, and sat up. In the shadows an amorphous figure swayed side to side, as if from one foot to the other. Simon squinted to make sense of the broad shoulders, absurdly thin body, and shortened arms. It looked like some fantastic tribal costume.

The movement stilled and the shape melted away. Simon fell back on his bed, inhaling a long, slow breath to compose himself. He hated waking this deep into the night. The sudden consciousness always confused him. What was dream and what was reality? He took another breath, sipping in air until his lungs couldn't hold any more, then exhaling slowly. A musky breeze billowed through the open window. The night was growing a little cooler, another storm blowing up the coast. It was an unusual pattern for July.

He curled on his side and reached out with his arm. It fell into the empty space next to him. That scared him for a moment. Amy was gone. Davey, too. The only life in the house was him, and Casper, sleeping in some soft spot. The illumined numbers on the alarm clock clicked away another minute of his life, 1:15 turning into 1:16. The night would get no darker.

Simon shifted onto his back again. A gust of wind spilled into the room, and the human figure in the shadows seemed to dance.

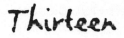 Thirteen

He dresses in black, head to toe, with a light cap tilted low over his eyes. He leaves the inn by the side door at midnight. No one sees him. He feels invisible, drained of flesh, consciousness without body. A few cars pass him on the way into town, and he wonders what the drivers perceive of him when they glance over.

He parks across the street and observes the house. There's little to note, just a single light on in the upstairs front window. After a while a shadow passes by, and the light extinguishes. He waits a suitable while longer, then gets out of the car. He strolls across the street and up the walk, in no hurry. He doesn't bother trying the front door this time, just continues around the side. The lights next door are out, the neighbors asleep. He turns the backdoor knob. It opens.

He listens—no dog barking, no noise at all. He steps into the kitchen and lets his eyes adjust to the dim light from some appliance on the counter. He has a choice now, turn back or continue? He continues across the kitchen toward the doorway, hesitates, then passes down the hallway to the staircase. He turns there and puts his foot on the first step. No squeaking, a solid stair covered with a thick rug. He climbs carefully, holding on to the railing. He counts as he goes, one to eleven, an unusually steep incline. At the top he looks right, into a small room with a bed against the wall. No one there. He moves on down the hall to the end where there's another door wide open. He leans his head around the doorjamb. In the bed a body breathes, the sheet rising and falling every few seconds, the tranquil rest of someone without a care in the world. He hears air expelling from the lungs, then sucked back in again. The rhythm of it relaxes him a little, and he soon finds himself breathing in synchrony. He feels oddly peaceful, as if sleeping himself. He has already gone further than he ever imagined he could. It thrills him to be doing this, floating through the house like a phantom. He has never felt so light, almost immaterial. It's a surprisingly pleasant sensation. He should leave, of course, before some misstep triggers a chain of events he can't control. But he wants to see the man in his most artless state. One cannot pose in sleep. He crosses the threshold into the bedroom and glides over the hardwood floor rather than lifting his weight and putting it down again. He stops a few feet from the bed and stares. The image soon emerges from the darkness—the low hairline, the thin lips, the nose straight and narrow. An appealing face, as it was as a boy. Everything so symmetrical.

The chest heaves, and he steps behind the clothes stand. The body rises up, seems to look around, then falls back on the bed. After a few minutes, the breathing becomes regular again, and he reappears from the shadows. On the dresser he sees a letter opener, with its long, thin blade. He picks it up in the soft leather of his glove. The body stirs in the bed, the arms shaking, as if tied down. He muffles his own breath with his hand and leans over. He sees the eyeballs fluttering under their lids, the reflection of dreaming. Of what? He feels an odd desire to know, to rouse the sleeper from his sleep and ask what he dreams of. Falling down a flight of stairs, perhaps, something cliché like that, a mind on the verge of giving in to its deepest urges. Or perhaps just a confusion of images, the random firings of a restless brain. Still, there could be meaning in what seems like chaos, if one looks long enough.

Then what would the disturber of dreams do—run? Thrust the knife? It would surprise him to find he's capable of doing that, but who would have predicted that he could go this far? A gust of wind brushes through the trees outside and bursts into the room, whipping the thin blue curtains against the window frame. The sudden cool air shivers his bare arms. The temperature is dropping, a cold front moving in as predicted. Why wouldn't a person lower the window on his way to bed? Didn't he listen to the eleven o'clock forecast? A careful man takes note of the changing weather and adjusts his window for the temperature that would come, not that already is.

His hand eases its grip on the knife. His arm hangs limply against the leg, the blade pointing downward, harmless. The fleeting impulse to kill evaporates from his consciousness. He has come tonight just to satisfy his curiosity—he might even admit that it is an obsession. The letter opener lying on the bureau was pure coincidence. It could have been put away in a drawer, mixed in with pads and pens, or not existed at all in this particular place. Then the thought of killing would not have occurred to him. Plunging a blade, even a dull one, into someone shouldn't be a matter of circumstance.

And so the uninvited visitor leaves as he has come, with silent footsteps. He glances into the room across the hall again. A light circle of fur rests against the pillow at the top of the bed. He admires the way cats above all species can ignore the comings and goings of humans that don't concern them. It would be relaxing not to pay attention. He resists the temptation to go in and pet the animal. He has already stayed longer than is perhaps wise. He regrets not having the time to see more of the house—the layout of the downstairs, the angles and spaces. He appreciates the softness of the carpet under his feet and the dim overhead light as he descends the stairs. His own apartment is so cold and bright. He leaves the letter opener on the bottom step, pushed under the rug, where the bulge of it may be noticed in a day or two. An experienced intruder wouldn't purposely disturb the scene, of course. There would remain on the carpet the faint imprints of his shoes—a common size—and in the air, linger the scent of some mild soap, not easily named. Otherwise not a trace.

Stepping out into the mist, he flips up the collar to his jacket. The slight bite to the air makes his skin shiver. He feels good realizing that he doesn't have to do anything drastic right away. Violating the sanctity of this man's home is enough, at least for one cool, moist night.

Fourteen

Summer carnival wad coming to Red Paint. Simon watched from his desk as workers set up the two rows of blue canvas tents, creating a makeshift midway. It amazed him how quickly they could turn the Common into an amusement park. In three days would come its destruction, leaving no trace of it beyond marks in the grass as the carnival moved on to a neighboring town.

He sensed movement toward his desk and looked up. A short, husky man dressed in jeans and red plaid shirt had his hand out. "Dan LeBeau. We met at a Chamber lunch a few months ago. I own LeBeau's Hardware."

Simon took the hand in an awkward grip, palm to fingers, and let go quickly. "Right, Dan," he said as if having a clear memory of the man. People expected

REUNION AT RED PAINT BAY

to be remembered by the editor of their town paper. "What can I do for you?"

LeBeau glanced about the newsroom. In the corner Carole was typing into her computer, her headphones on. He nodded her way. "Your police reporter, she called me for her story."

"What story is that?"

"I've got a finance manager, Bonnie, been with me for eight years. I found out this week she's been stealing from me. It started out small, a few hundred dollars here and there. Then it got to moving thousands of dollars at a time into fake accounts, pretending to pay bills."

"So you turned her in to the police, and Carole has the copy?"

"Yeah, but you can't run the story."

"We *can't*?"

"It'll kill my reputation around here."

Simon wrapped up the remains of his tuna sandwich and glanced out the window. A long truck marked WORLD'S BEST MOBILE PETTING ZOO pulled up on Mechanic Street. There were no windows in the huge vehicle, which made him wonder, did North American Traveling Amusements Inc. treat its animals humanely? He could assign someone to go undercover and find out—Rigero, maybe, as an itinerant worker. But if the story closed down the carnival, the *Register* would never be forgiven.

"So," LeBeau said, "you can understand my position."

As far as Simon could tell, that position boiled down to *I'll be embarrassed, so you can't run the story.* "From my experience, readers always sympathize with the injured party," he said. "They may be surprised you didn't catch on sooner, but they won't blame you. They'll think you're a good guy who got taken advantage of."

LeBeau stepped closer to the desk. "Who's going to buy paints and brushes from somebody who can't keep track of tens of thousands of dollars? Some people already think I'm soaking them."

"Are you?" The question was abrupt, but Simon was glad he said it in just that way. He had bought from LeBeau's many times.

LeBeau cocked his head. "You charge what people are willing to pay. That's the way it works."

"It works that way because you have no competition. You have what, three stores?"

"Four. We just opened in Rawley."

"So you have the only four hardware stores within thirty miles of here."

LeBeau looked out of the window for a moment, conjuring his next argument. "Look, I'm a private company. My financial numbers are nobody's business. I'm not pressing charges against Bonnie. We're going to work it out between us."

Simon glanced over at Carole. "I'm afraid you made it public the moment you called the police."

LeBeau picked up the snow globe on Simon's desk and shook it. Little flakes of white floated through the liquid, landing on the small skyline of Portland. "I advertise in the *Register*," he said. "I was thinking of doing a big promotion for our new store."

Simon stood up. "Advertising and editorial are separate departments, Dan. We can't pick and choose what to run from the police log. It's often embarrassing to someone, even advertisers."

"I didn't see you running a picture of the graffiti on your door a week ago. Wasn't that news, somebody scrawling *RAPIST* on the front door of the *Register*?" He said the word louder than the rest, and even Carole with her earphones in looked over.

"You're getting desperate now."

LeBeau tossed the snow globe between his hands. "A lot of folks around here would like to know if our friendly little town paper is hiding a sexual predator."

Simon moved toward the door, inducing LeBeau to follow. "We're not hiding anything, Dan. But we do have a reputation to keep up for reporting all the local news, not just some of it."

"Right, you make your reputation by ruining mine. That make you feel good?"

It was his job to report the news, regardless of whom it hurt. Journalists did that every day all over

the country. What did he feel about it—proud, satisfied, sorry at times?

LeBeau dropped the plastic globe in Simon's hand.
"I didn't think you'd have an answer for that."

As Simon turned into the driveway of his home, there
was the Volvo, parked slightly crooked, Amy's trade-
mark. He pushed in the front door and saw her black
sandals in the hallway, as if she had stepped out of them
midstride. It always relieved him to see the tracks of
her around the house.

"Amy?"

There was silence for a few seconds, then: "In here."

He hurried to the kitchen where she was standing at the sink, opening a can. He wrapped his arms
around her and she twisted her head so that their
cheeks rubbed against each other. He loved the smooth
feel of her skin, unlike any other sensation he could
think of. It was pure Amy.

She checked her watch. "You're home early."

"That's because I'm taking you out on the town
tonight."

"Which town?"

"Red Paint, of course. The carnival is back."

She shifted around inside his arms to face him.
"You get like a little kid this time every summer."

"If you can't get excited when you go to a carnival, you must be dead."

She pulled back slightly. "Davey stays with us this year, no running off on his own."

"He is eleven, Amy."

"Eleven going on eight."

Simon leaned in for a kiss and tasted something different—new lipstick? New toothpaste? "We don't kiss much anymore," he said when they broke apart. "Why is that?"

"I haven't been keeping score," she said and then kissed him again, "but you can add one more to our total." She turned away, toward the refrigerator. "When you go upstairs, tell Davey to wash for dinner. I'm throwing together a vegetable soup. It's all I have the energy to make."

Simon headed down the hallway, grabbing his briefcase as he went, and turned up the stairs. At the top he stopped outside his son's room, listening for a moment. Not spying really, more information gathering, as he'd do in the bank or supermarket, trying to pick up on what people were talking about. He heard an unfamiliar voice on the other side of the door, lower-pitched and slower-paced than Davey's usual rapid-fire delivery. He tried to distinguish words but could only make out "Yeah" and "Nah." He knocked. Nothing. He waited a few seconds and knocked again, harder.

Still nothing. Simon nudged open the door and peeked around it. "Davey?"

The boy sat cross-legged on his bed, propped up by pillows, the phone at one ear, his earbud in the other. "I got to get off now," he said with exaggerated loudness, "on account of my father has invaded my room." He hung up the receiver.

"It's time for dinner, and afterward we're all going to the carnival together."

The boy's face contorted into a mixture of disbelief and resignation. "You mean I have to go with you guys?"

"Mom's orders. Go with us or not at all."

Small white lights stretched between the trees down both sides of the Common, illuminating the green as if it were a large rectangular stage suspended in the black of space. The air burst with sounds of a banjo band and kids yelling and one strong-lunged baby crying. They walked down the crowded midway, bumped and brushed at every step. Simon reached ahead to tap Amy's shoulder. "This is the most crowded I've ever seen it," he said. "You can barely move."

She licked her chocolate cone. "Where's Davey?"

He looked back into the swirling lights of the Merry-Go-Round, trying to pick out the slight form of their son. "By that booth with the water guns," Simon said, vaguely pointing. "Around there."

"You see him?"

"Not this second, but—"

"You said you were watching him."

Simon rose up on his toes, looking for the telltale blue cap. "Okay, I see him. But this is ridiculous. We can't keep our eyes on him every second just because we spooked ourselves one time."

She moved in closer so he could hear her. "I didn't spook myself. The person Davey saw at the front door spooked me."

"It could have just been somebody coming around selling something."

"At eight o'clock on a Thursday night? And why didn't he ring the bell?" They'd gone over this before. He didn't have all the answers. "A carnival is exactly where predators hang out and snatch kids," she said.

"If he's not safe in the center of Red Paint, we might as well move to Canada."

Amy gestured with her cone toward the tent. "What's he doing now?"

A quizzical expression flashed across Simon's face before he could stop it. "He's just talking to someone."

"Who?"

"I can't tell from here, some man maybe."

"A man?" Amy pushed her way against the tide of people. "Davey!" she yelled with an urgency in her voice that made everyone stop and look. Twenty yards away, the boy waved and waded into the crowd toward them. For a moment they lost sight of him, then he popped up next to them.

"Hey Mom, can I—"

"What did that man want?"

"What man?"

She motioned toward the tent, but there was only a mass of backs, no one distinguishable. "The man you were just talking to."

"I don't know."

"Then why were you talking to him?"

"He said hello, so I said hello back. You told me to be polite to people."

"Is he the father of one of your friends?"

"Maybe."

"Maybe?"

"I think so, 'cause he knew my name, except he called me David."

"He knew your name?"

"Yeah, so?"

"What else did he say?"

"I don't remember. Can I have six bucks to go on the bumper cars? Please."

"The bumper cars don't cost six dollars," Simon said.

"Three rides do."

Amy took two dollars from her pocketbook, and Davey grabbed them. "Thanks."

"We'll come watch you," she said.

Davey twisted up his face in yet another expression of disgust. He seemed to have an endless variety of ways to show his revulsion. "Dad?"

Simon had thought about going on the ride as well, renewing their battle from last year when they rammed each other at every turn. This year, it seemed, Davey wanted to be on his own.

"How about we watch him get on," Simon said to Amy, "and then we go away till he's done?"

As Davey ran off a young man stepped in front of them. His face was unshaven and his curly hair spread wildly across his head. Amy grabbed Simon's arm.

"Mr. Howe," the fellow said, grinning now, which exposed two sharp canine teeth, as if they had been filed to a point. "It's me, Randy—you know, the Hero of Dakin Road."

"Right, Randy Caine," Simon said, his body un-stiffening. "I didn't recognize you from your mug shots."

"Yeah, they never get my best side."

Amy nudged him with her elbow. Of course he should introduce her, but to Randy Caine? If she never wanted to meet David the rapist, what would she think of Randy, the inveterate small-time trouble-maker? "Amy, this is Randy Caine. He's graced our pages a few times."

She put out her hand, which seemed to take Randy by surprise. He wiped his right hand on the sleeve of his left arm and then took hers for a powerful shake.

"Nice to meet you, Mrs. Howe. Your husband, he always makes me look good."

"That was a daring thing you did," Simon said, "rescuing the girl from the fire. It deserved page one. Sorry we only had your mug shot on file."

"That's okay. Everybody says I'm like Superman or something. Feels funny, you know, being a hero."

"It was a bit out of character."

Amy looked over at him as if he was being rude, but Randy nodded amiably. "You won't catch me doing nothing like that again. I mean, cops patting me on the back, people stopping to shake my hand. The next person comes up to me . . ."

"We all have our crosses to bear," Simon said so Randy wouldn't have to finish his threat, "for better or worse."

"Definitely for worse," Randy said and backed away into the crowd.

After the bumper cars, Davey coaxed them to the Hall of Mirrors. "Not me," Amy said. "I don't need to see myself coming and going."

"Then you have to come with me, Dad."

"I don't know," Simon said, feigning reluctance, and Davey grabbed his hand and pulled him to the entrance. The boy handed over two tickets and plunged ahead, banging hard into the first mirror he came to.

"Careful," Simon said, "you'll break the glass."

"It's unbreakable," Davey said, punching at it to demonstrate. Then he reached up with his hands to cover his father's face. "Close your eyes."

"I'm not doing this with my eyes closed."

"Just close them and spin around and then go through. I'm doing it, too."

Simon closed his eyes and felt Davey's small hands on his waist, turning him. After two revolutions he looked. His son was gone.

"Davey?" Simon turned about, groped the air ahead of him, touched glass, and turned again. "Where are you?"

The boy's head stuck out sideways from the edge of the mirrors, as if floating. Hands came out, gripped the skinny neck. His tongue dropped from his mouth, his eyes widened, and then his head was yanked away.

"Very funny," Simon said. "Now stay where you are until I catch up." He stepped forward carefully, hit glass, turned and hit glass again. *Okay, this isn't possible. There has to be a way forward.* He reached ahead and touched glass, and when he did a man appeared there, but ahead or behind, Simon couldn't tell. He thought about asking which way to go, or just following, but the person wasn't moving. And which man would he ask from the dozens around him?

"Davey?" Simon said, then louder, "Davey?"

"Lose someone?" The voice sounded soothing, the god of the Hall of Mirrors checking in on his realm.

But a god with a baseball cap pulled halfway down his face.

"Did a boy pass you?"

"A slender boy about ten or eleven, with sandy hair?"

Simon stared at the fractured images. "Yes."

They smiled, a hundred smiling faces.

"I did see him. You're very lucky to have a beautiful boy like that."

Beautiful. Simon moved forward a few feet, banged into glass.

The man laughed. "Take your time," he said, "and don't trust your eyes." Then he was gone.

The only image Simon could see now was his own, ten Simons, and when he moved a little, a hundred of them. All Simon. No Davey. "Davey!" he shouted. He began to rush ahead, sweeping the air, turning and turning until suddenly he found empty space. It was as if the maze had suddenly disappeared. There was only one way to go and he had found it, the magic path. Soon he heard sounds of the outside, the familiar organ music, and he felt fresh air in his face. In a few moments he was outside, standing behind the Hall of Mirrors, across from the Register Building. There was Davey, bent over tying his sneakers.

The boy looked up. "What took you so long?"

———

Simon didn't tell Amy about the stranger in the Hall of Mirrors. What would he say, that a man in there spoke of Davey as a "beautiful boy"? She might get hysterical, if he could use that word, and not let their son out of her sight.

Simon steered them down the midway toward the exit. Halfway there he said, "That's it for tonight, kiddo. Mom and I both have work tomorrow."

"Just one more ride," Davey said in his familiar pleading voice. No matter what the occasion, he always asked for once more.

Simon glanced at the amusements within eyeshot— the Ferris wheel, the Catapult, and just a little farther ahead, the Teacups, closest to the exit. "Okay, you can go on the Teacups once, then we leave." He handed over two dollars and Davey ran ahead, with both of them keeping him in sight. When they reached the entrance the boy was already circling the ride, picking his seat. They saw him open the metal restraining door and climb in. In a moment, the Teacups began to move.

"I never liked this ride," Amy said as she slipped her hand in Simon's and leaned on the railing. "Too much bumping into people."

"That's the point," he said, "bumping into your friends as hard as you can."

They watched as the different-colored cups spun around on their axes, and the whole ride spun as well. It was dizzying to look at.

"I've lost track," Amy said. "Which one is Davey in?"

Simon pointed to the left, but by the time she turned there, the car had rotated away. "The red one, I think, coming toward us."

The red teacup spun in front of them, and there was Davey shouting at them, his face contorted into a crazy grin, his arms waving. Next to him, his mouth open as if frozen that way, was a man. The teacup spun away.

Amy squeezed Simon's arm. "Did you see him?"

"Yes," Simon said, "he looked like he was having fun."

"I meant the man. There's a grown man riding the Teacups with Davey."

They focused on the red cup, and when it came toward them again, only the back was visible, no faces. Amy pulled Simon sideways a few steps to get a better view, but in a moment it was gone.

The Teacups picked up speed. They flew around the circle and spun on their axes. Davey came into view again, this time flung toward the outside of the cup, pinned against the man, almost in his lap.

"Oh God."

"He's in plain view, Amy."

In a minute the ride began to slow. Simon watched the red cup, trying to judge where it would stop, and moved counterclockwise around the railing to meet it. Just a few yards ahead of him Davey jumped to the ground. The man was just behind him.

"Davey?" Simon called, but the boy didn't hear, or didn't let on that he did. He walked with the man toward the exit on the far side of the ride, looking up once or twice, as if talking. When he passed through the gate he turned and came running toward them. "Can I do it again, Dad?"

"Who was that in the car with you?" Simon said.

Davey glanced back. "I don't know, some man."

"Did he touch you?"

"Touch me?"

"It looked like he was touching you," Amy said, coming up behind them.

"It's the Teacups, Mom. You can't help touching people."

"Did he say anything?"

"I don't know, he was yelling like me. Everybody was yelling. Can't I ride again, Mom?"

"We're going home," she said, taking Davey's hand.

He yanked it away. "What are you doing?"

"It's time to go," Simon said, giving their son a little shove.

Fifteen

He leans against the back of the sausage truck, inhaling the smell of cooked meats as he watches the front gate. He doesn't need to hide. Paul Chambers doesn't really exist, and no one would recognize him as Paul Walker even if they had been in the same class or lived on the same street. His face has filled out like the rest of him, and his hair receded. He doesn't wear glasses anymore. He does have a thin mustache and one slightly drooping eyelid, as if he has recovered only partially from an early-age stroke. Altogether unrecognizable, he's sure. And unexpected. It wouldn't occur to anyone to ask, *What do you think Paul Walker is up to these days?* No one would wonder if he were in Red Paint. No one would care.

An hour passes as it does when one is waiting, ago-
nizingly slowly. That's how it was waiting for Jean at
this same spot the summer after junior year. He was
sure that she wouldn't come, sure that he had misinterpreted her mumbled assent to meet him at seven at the
carnival. And then there she was, fifteen minutes late, in
a sleeveless dress that billowed out from her legs at the
slightest breeze. He wanted to stroll arm in arm with
her down the midway, but she said she felt out of place
with all the other girls in shorts. He steered her to the
dimly lit outer path, the back side of the amusements,
wondering if she just didn't want to be seen with him.
He had money and offered her ice cream or a lobster
sandwich or soda. She said no thanks to everything.
She did agree to a ride and chose the Ferris wheel.
Their car stopped at the very top, and from there they
gazed over the lights of Red Paint, trying to pick out
their own houses. As she looked over the side he put his
hand on her knee, just below the hem of her dress. He
moved his fingers a little, then the wheel moved again.

He feels foolish waiting now. Perhaps they arrived
early and were already wandering the grounds. They
could be coming on one of the other two nights of the
carnival. Just as he pushes himself away from the
truck he spots Simon walking through the gate, his
wife by his side. A minute or two later and he would
have missed them. Is this how finely God plans things,
everything happening just in time?

They're holding hands, an intimate act. Palms pressed against each other. Fingers intertwined. *We belong to each other.* That's what holding hands announces to the world. *We have each other to go home with and hold and kiss. Who do you have?*

"Come on, Davey," Simon calls over his shoulder, and the boy runs the few yards to catch up, an obedient son. *Davey.*

Paul bends over as if to wipe something off his shoe as they pass him by. Then he follows them down the midway a few steps behind, plenty of people in between.

He has always loved the Hall of Mirrors, the feeling that one could dissolve into them, linger there and watch, then reappear at will. Or not reappear at all. He stares into the mirror now, hands on his hips, and it stares back, blank. Perhaps just a faint outline of where a body should be, the hint of presence, the impression of a form just passing through. He hears footsteps, stands still, waits. Then a voice making a kind of whacking sound. In a moment the boy turns the corner, his eyes closed, punching ahead of himself. His small fist lands in Paul's belly, and his eyes flash open. "Sorry mister, I didn't mean to hit you."

"It's okay," Paul says, letting his hand fall reassuringly on the boy's shoulder. "I used to do this with my eyes closed, too, when I was your age. I guess there are two of us who know the trick."

"The trick?"

"With your eyes closed the mirrors can't fool you."

Davey squints up at him, the beginning of farsightedness. "Didn't I see you before?"

"Maybe. I've been around the carnival all night."

Davey takes a step, bumps into the glass hard, laughs, and then makes faces at himself. In the mirror a dozen boys are grinning madly.

Sixteen

A white ball of fur lay sprawled across the breakfast table, basking in the slanting light from the bay window. Amy sat on the bench, stroking Casper's head with one hand and holding a book in the other. Simon dropped a yellow legal pad on the table and slipped in on the opposite side. He poked the cat in the rear a few times with his pen. No response. "I gather we've given up trying to keep Casper off our eating surfaces."

"She does it all day when we're not here, so why bother?" Amy turned back to a bookmarked page. "What do you think of this? 'People only grow around sadness.'"

"Sounds right, I guess. Who said it?" Amy held up the book—*Semrad: The Heart of a Therapist*. He figured that he was supposed to know who Semrad was. She had probably mentioned him dozens of times.

"He mentored a generation of therapists in how to connect to their patients with their heart, not just their heads. But I think he got it backward. People don't grow when they're sad, they're too busy *being* sad. The same if people are angry or depressed or in pain—they get trapped in these emotions."

"You're disagreeing with the eminent Semrad?"

"Daring, aren't I?"

Simon wrote on his pad, and Amy let her book close over her finger. "Doing your column?"

"I'm taking to heart your suggestion that the post-card sender is a threat and making a list of all the peo-ple who might want to fold, spindle, or mutilate me." He scribbled a name, and Amy leaned across the table to see.

"Who's Ray Jefferson?"

"My first roommate after college. I told him he had to move out after his year was up."

"Why did you do that?"

Simon tried to project back to his former self. "He seemed fake to me. He'd say things like, 'I love the smell of winter, don't you?' and 'Making music is like making love'—that's another one. He was pretending to be sensitive."

"Maybe he thought you'd like that about him."

"Why would I care how sensitive he was?"

Amy shrugged. "Sensitivity is one of those positive qualities a person can have."

"Not to a twenty-two-year-old male it isn't."

"Wait—he wasn't gay, was he?"

"No, I didn't kick him out because he was gay or I thought he was gay, if that's what you're asking."

"So how did he react?"

Simon remembered the expression on Ray's face, a strange mixture of embarrassment and disbelief with a dose of hatred. "He said he'd fall apart if I kicked him out, and I guess he did for a while, with cocaine, went to jail for eighteen months. I can imagine him blaming me."

Amy reached her hand to stroke Casper, and the cat stretched out, exposing her belly. "You think twenty years later he'd still be blaming you?"

"I don't know," Simon said. "He *was* the kind to carry a grudge."

When Simon called Davey for dinner, the boy came rushing down the steps as always, one misstep away from plunging headlong into the front door. At the bottom he grabbed the post to turn into the hallway, and Simon saw a thin metal handle jutting from his back pocket. "Hold on, what's that?"

Davey twisted around to see. "What?"

"Is that a knife?"

He pulled it out. "No, it's a letter opener."

"A letter opener is a knife."

The boy rubbed his finger along the blade. "Not when it's this crappy. It couldn't cut soup."

Simon put out his palm, and Davey handed it over, blade first. "Why did you take this off my bureau?"

"Why would I take your stupid old letter opener?"

"That's what I'm asking you."

"I found it on the stairs, okay? It was sticking out from the rug." He pointed to the spot. "You shouldn't leave your knife lying around like that, Dad, 'cause I could have stepped on it with my bare feet and got lockjaw."

"I didn't leave it on the steps, Davey."

"Does your jaw really lock when you get lockjaw?"

"It can, if you don't get a tetanus shot."

"Then I better eat dinner fast." He started for the kitchen.

"Wait, you didn't take this out anywhere, did you?"

Davey hesitated. "Not really."

"What does that mean?"

"I put the knife in my pocket and kind of forgot it was there when I went to Kenny's."

"Don't tell me you took it out at Kenny's."

"Okay, I won't."

"Davey, did you take it out?"

"Not really."

"Will you stop saying that? You either did or didn't take it out."

"It sort of fell out when we were fooling around."

"Did you put it somewhere safe when it fell out?"

"Sure, Dad. You think I want to get sliced open by accident?"

"I don't know what you're thinking anymore."

"Yeah, I'm kind of a mystery," Davey said. "Can I go eat now?"

"Go," Simon said as he stared at a place on the steps where the rug was pushed up a little, exactly where Davey had pointed.

In bed that night, the yellow pad propped against his knees, he added to his possible threats. There seemed to be no end to the people who might want to do him in.

Amy let *Semrad* drop on her chest. "Your list is growing."

"Eleven so far."

"You can think of eleven people who might want to harm you?"

"Like you said, I'm the editor of a newspaper and apparently I have a knack for pissing people off." He wrote down a twelfth name—Dana Maines.

Amy tilted the gooseneck lamp to shine on his pad. "What did you do to Dana?"

"We were going to take off to L.A. together after we graduated from Bowdoin. She wanted to be an actress, and I was going to write screenplays she could star in."

"Sounds like you had it all planned out."

"Yeah, well, everything seemed possible, if you got out of Maine first. But then I heard she was telling people we were eloping, and getting married was the last thing I wanted to do, since I was waiting for the perfect girl to come along." He tapped Amy on her arm. "So I screwed up my courage and went to the coffee shop where we were meeting and told her I wasn't going."

"How did she take it?"

Simon pushed up the sleeve to his shirt and pointed at several small indentations just below his left shoulder. "She stabbed me with a fork."

"I thought that was from a vaccination."

"It's from Dana. She got really loud saying how I was backing out on her and ruining her dreams. I reached over to quiet her down, and she stabbed me."

"Bit of an overreaction."

"I thought so. Anyway, I saw a note in the *Bowdoin Alumni News* a couple of weeks ago that she's moved back to Portland. I was going to drive over there this week for Jack Monroe's retirement party from the

Herald, so I thought I'd look her up and see if she could be the one sending me weird postcards. She was definitely the type."

"We decided the sender is male."

"If your theory of penmanship is right, yes."

"You sure you're not just looking for an excuse to meet up with an old flame?"

"You're the only old flame in my life." He turned toward her to kiss, and as they did he shoved the yellow pad to the floor so that nothing would come between them.

Seventeen

Paul Chambers Walker leans into the stiff breeze. It invigorates him, the feel of it against his face. To the east he can see a patch of blue between the distant trees, and he's sure it's the ocean. So many things are like that, he thinks, recognizable if you already know what you are looking at.

He turns to the small, square office building and scans the list of tenants. There she is—Amelia Howe, second floor. He pushes in the glass doors and takes the broad steps by twos. The first office at the top of the stairs has a gold-plated sign, LEVIN AND HOWE. He enters the waiting room, empty as he expected it would be at the end of the day. It's a messy area, with the cheap blue vinyl chairs out of line and magazines scattered across the coffee table. The large plant in the corner is yellowing and dropping leaves. The inner office door opens and Amy Howe appears, her shoes in her hand. Her hair is pulled back, all business. Close up she seems younger than he thought from the quick glimpses at the carnival, and prettier, perhaps.

She balances on one leg and then the other to slip on her shoes. "I didn't know anyone was out here."

"I didn't mean to surprise you," he says.

"You must be the one who called about a five o'clock appointment."

He nods over his shoulder. "You're overwatering the plant. You'll kill it that way."

"Thanks. I'll watch that."

She looks him up and down without moving her head, just the slightest shifting of her eyes, a talent she must have honed over years of assessing clients for whatever small mark or twitch that might hint at what is troubling them. They are alone here, a man and a woman. Does she feel their isolation as he does?

She holds out her right hand. "I'm Amy Howe."

He takes it and shakes repeatedly, squeezing a little harder each time. "Paul Chambers, Dr. Howe."

"Actually, I'm an LIC SW—a licensed social worker."

"Sorry."

She slides her hand gently from his. "I don't normally see clients at this hour, Mr. Chambers. My last appointment is three to four."

He smiles a bit sheepishly. "Your service said they would have to check with you about it, and since I didn't hear back, I figured I'd come over."

"They tried to reach you. The number you left seems to be wrong."

"Really?" he says with the appropriate amount of surprise to his voice. "I'm staying over at the Bayswater Inn. Maybe I got the number mixed up. I do that sometimes, I have to confess, a bit of dyslexia with figures. If this is inconvenient for you, I'll make an appointment for another time, of course."

She looks indulgently at him, ready to make an exception for a poor soul who can't even get a simple phone number right. What threat can there be from a man who so willingly offers to leave?

"Since you're here," she says, "please come in."

Paul moves past her into the office and sits in the leather chair. He runs his hands over the smooth brown hide of the arm, back and forth, skin against skin. She goes behind her desk and pulls out a pad. He scans the wall and sees her professional certificate, University of Maine, Orono. A state school.

"May I call you Paul?"

"I prefer Mr. Chambers."

"Okay, Mr. Chambers, what brings you here?"

Her directness appeals to him, no preliminary questions of who he is and where he comes from. Just *What brings you here?* "I'm having dangerous thoughts."

His answer doesn't throw her. No reaction at all, except for letting the pen slide between her fingers and tapping it against her desk, then turning it over and tapping again. Nervousness or stalling? Perhaps a former smoker needing continual stimulation of her fingertips. "What kind of dangerous thoughts?"

"What kind?"

"Your thoughts could be about some thing or person or yourself."

"Some person."

"How frequently are you having these thoughts?"

"Every day." She writes this down on her pad. "Many times a day," he adds. She writes this, too. "Virtually every moment." He has her attention now, so why not go all the way? "I even dream dangerous thoughts," he says. Surely that makes him a very dangerous person, doesn't it? He leans back in his chair into the drift of cool air coming from the vent in the ceiling. It tickles his nose and makes him sneeze as he always does, three quick times.

"God bless you," Amy says.

He pulls out his handkerchief to rub his nose. "Catholic."

"Excuse me?"

"Catholics say God bless you. During the plague the pope ordered people to say that when somebody sneezed because a sneeze was supposed to expel the soul from the body."

"I'm not Catholic, Mr. Chambers."

"Not now, no, but how were you raised?"

She opens her mouth as if to answer, then looks down at her pad. He takes this opportunity to size up the small rectangular office, noting its spareness, its utility. There's nothing diverting on her desk—no Buckyballs or Rubik's Cube or magnetic puzzles to occupy one's hands. On the walls, nothing to distract a patient. A thick curtain covers the window. It is the space of a no-nonsense person.

She says, "The dangerous thoughts that you're concerned about, are you acting on them in any way?"

If he answers yes she'll undoubtedly inquire as to what actions he has taken. If he answers no she'll presume he's just talk. He knows the drill. "Maybe."

She shakes her head. "I don't understand *maybe*."

Of course she doesn't. Ambivalence isn't allowed here. He's either acting on his dangerous thoughts or he isn't. He's either crazy or he isn't. He's either justified in his actions or he isn't.

"It's a long story," he says. "How shall I begin?"

Eighteen

Simon wasn't surprised to see the story slugged *Randy Caine Arrested Again* appear in his news inbox. It was only a matter of time before Red Paint's resident troublemaker reverted to form. He had a reputation to keep up, and he certainly wasn't going to let himself be defined by some errant impulse to do good for once in his life. Simon clicked on the story and read:

Police Nab Suspect in
B&E at Flaubert's

Randall Caine, hailed last month as a hero for pulling a local girl from a burning car on Dakin Road, was

arrested Saturday at 10:52 p.m. for breaking and enter-
ing in the nighttime.

Police say Caine, 27, was caught in the alley next to
Flaubert's Spa carrying a crowbar, with a glass cutter
concealed on his person. The door to Red Paint's popu-
lar market was found forced open. It is not known yet
what items, if any, were missing.

According to police, Caine said that at the time of his
arrest he found the crowbar in the alley and was looking
for a phone to use to report the open door.

Off the top of his head, Simon could recall at least
five other such stories since he'd become editor—Caine
nabbed for possessing marijuana, Caine stopped for
driving without a license, Caine inciting the Tiger Tav-
ern melee, Caine breaking a restraining order, Caine
threatening a lawyer (his own). The youngest member
of Red Paint's first family of crime was determined to
make his own mark in town. Simon deleted the headline
and wrote: *Hero of Car Accident Arrested on Burglary Charge.*
In the notes field of the file he typed, "Box on Page 1."
Randy always appreciated the prominent placement.

He did phone Dana Maines, and after a few minutes of
catching up suggested lunch in Portland. She agreed
so enthusiastically that he felt compelled to mention
Amy for the first time in their conversation.

"You're married?" she said.

"Sixteen years."

"And you're calling me up?"

"I thought we could have lunch."

"Why?"

The question stymied him. He could hardly say he wanted to make sure she wasn't stalking him, and he certainly didn't want to give the impression he was interested in hooking up. "You're right," he said, "there really is no reason for us to have lunch."

"Okay then," she said and hung up.

It happened so quickly he didn't even have time to ask if she had made it to California.

Nineteen

When Paul settles into the leather armchair again, he feels the warmth of the body just gone. He wonders what poor person recently sat there pouring out his miseries as if they were the trials of Job. Misery always seems that way to the afflicted—unbearable, unimaginable, unlike anything anyone else has ever experienced. But who would trade the misery he knows for the misery of others? No one passed him in the waiting room going out. So how did the distressed person leave, through a secret exit for those who can't stand to be seen? He feels the weight of this invisible stranger all about, a thick layer of him on the desktop, like fine dust, piles of him on the carpet, and the pungent odor of him soaking the air. In one hour here he would have sloughed off a couple of million cells, shedding his outermost self flake by flake. Paul inhales long and deep, breathing the stranger inside him.

"Mr. Chambers," Amy Howe says, going by him and around her desk, "sorry to keep you waiting."

Then why has she? Why show him into her office and then go out into the waiting room—to do what, see if her colleague Dr. Levin will stay around in case there's trouble with the mysterious new client? It doesn't make sense, people apologizing for what they could easily do differently.

He says, "Do you know why misery loves company?"

She takes her seat without response, not willing to say whether she does or doesn't know.

"Because it needs an audience."

She nods at his observation. "I'll have to give that more thought." But apparently not right now. "In our first session Monday," she says, "we talked about the thoughts that were bothering you, and we'll continue that in a moment. But I want to start by getting some basic information."

"No," Paul says.

"No?"

He has her attention, all of it, in the slight tilt of her head, the wide-open eyes, the tongue hesitating just inside her lips. He takes out his handkerchief and rubs across his nose, prolonging the moment. "My thoughts don't bother me, like you said. I'm just constantly aware of them. Actually, I find them very interesting."

"Okay, we'll get into that. Have you sought help or counseling before?"

He notices that her right eye stretches out wider than the left, as if it has been pinched back by a finger molding clay, a slip of the hand by a lesser creator. Cosmetic surgery could probably correct the problem, if she considered it a problem at all. He regrets this tendency in himself, always seeing the small imperfections in people and wondering about their effect over a lifetime. What was her question?

"With a therapist or psychiatrist," she says, "or maybe a clergyman?"

"Yes."

"With . . . ?"

"A dog."

"Your dog?"

Paul coughs a little, letting his answer sink in, the peculiar psychological ramifications of it. There would be many. He sees a brown spot, slightly raised, on the right side of her face, only visible in a certain direct light. Cancerous, possibly. One in ten chance. Is it his place to mention the possibly lethal blemish? Would she be offended? "It was Jean's dog, actually, a border collie with a reddish brown coat and glacier blue eyes. Her name was Sadie."

"Are you putting me on here, Mr. Chambers?"

"I know it sounds ridiculous." There he is again, owning up to his eccentricity. Dangerously odd people don't do that because they're not aware of how dangerous they seem to others. Now to offer a perfectly reasonable explanation. "When Jean moved away she didn't want to take the dog from her familiar surroundings, so she left her with me. Sadie would curl up next to me on the sofa, sleep at the bottom of my bed, and I started talking to her. People do that, don't they, talk to their pets when there's no one else in the home?"

"It's probably not uncommon."

"You mean it's probably common?"

"If you prefer it that way."

"So I told Sadie about my thoughts, whatever came to mind. She didn't talk back, if that's what you're wondering. But she was a good listener, and it helped, I think."

"How did this dog—"

"Sadie."

"How did Sadie help you?"

He hasn't harmed anyone yet, for one thing. To all appearances he is a reasonably functioning human being, and aren't appearances the currency of the realm in the twenty-first century? He says, "It always helps to open up to someone, don't you think?" Of course she does, it's her job to be that someone.

"Your wife—"

"Jean."

"You intimated last time that Jean had died recently."

"Three weeks ago. Too many Seconals." Looking at it another way, she took exactly the right number of pills. Jean would have researched the required overdose very carefully.

"Was this intentional or accidental?"

"Jean was always very intentional," he says.

"Do you know why your wife committed suicide?"

He nods. How could a husband not know?

"Would you like to talk about the reason?"

"She hated herself."

"Why did she hate herself?"

"She wished to be a different person."

"What kind of person?"

"A person who could forget. That was Jean's burden, really, she remembered everything in great detail. Some people are like that. The secret to happiness is having a bad memory, don't you agree?"

She treats his question as rhetorical, which it wasn't. So many interesting threads of conversation like this get lost in the day.

"What did Jean remember?" she asks, back to her job of asking.

Paul stares at the brown spot, about an inch from her right eye. He wonders what a slice of that flesh would look like under the microscope. She flicks her hand over the area. A suggestible sort. "She remembered what was done to her."

"What was done to her?"

He nods at the spot. "You should really have that looked at."

"Excuse me?"

"On your face there, the discoloration. I wouldn't take any chances. I'd have that looked at."

"It's just a birthmark, Mr. Chambers. Now I'd like you to focus—"

"She was assaulted."

Her head leans toward him with interest, her eyes dilating. "I see," she says, even though she couldn't possibly, at least not yet. It's just something to say. "When did this assault take place?"

"Twenty-five years ago."

"Twenty-five years," she repeats.

"Too long?"

"That's not for me to judge. Some people get over traumatic events quickly, others bury the memories in their subconscious for many years. In a few people the pain turns into impacted grief that they live with for a lifetime. They actually can get very comfortable with it. It's the only self they know—the grieving self— especially if the incident happened at an early age before they've established their full identity."

Paul finds himself nodding, agreeing to everything she says. So eminently sensible. "What grief have you felt?"

Her head rises from her papers. "We're here to talk about you, Mr. Chambers, and your wife."

"Have you felt any grief at all?"

"Everyone has reason to grieve at times. Given the grief your wife couldn't escape, could she have felt death would be a release for her?"

"You mean that she'd be better off dead?" he asks, to be perfectly clear.

"Some people are comforted by the idea of moving on to a place where they don't suffer."

"Heaven," he says.

"That's one possibility."

"I've always wondered what a body would do forever in heaven. Hell is quite vivid in the Bible—chained head and foot in the lake of flames, the weeping and wailing. But heaven, nobody ever says what it would be like to exist there for a single day let alone forever. Tertullian tried, but I don't find his answer very satisfactory."

"Tertullian?"

"He was an early Christian philosopher. He said that one of the most intense pleasures in heaven would be to look down at the miseries people were suffering in hell. Personally, if that's all he can come up with, I'll take hell. At least there you're experiencing the real thing, not watching it."

She seems lost in the conversation, where to go from here. Perhaps he is getting carried away. He has that tendency. She says, "Was there a funeral?"

"Yes."

"And did you go?"

"Yes. It was very unsatisfying. Preachers don't know anything more about death than the rest of us. I walked out before the service was finished. Do you think that was disrespectful?"

"I'm sure the minister understood."

"I meant to Jean."

She rubs her eyes, taking a moment to think. "I'd say what's important is whether you feel you disrespected her."

"They left her bed unmade."

"Excuse me?"

"When I left the service," he says, "I went to her apartment to dispose of her things. The people from the funeral home, they didn't straighten up when they took Jean away." He can see the bed now in his mind, the white cotton blanket bunched up at the bottom, the sheets hanging off the side, her pillow on the floor. The mattress sagging in the middle, the imprint of a solitary sleeper. He remembers running his hands over the sheet as if tracing the shape of her—the curve of her legs, the bulk of her hips, her bony spine. His wife reduced to an impression in the bed, the memory of a mattress.

"That particularly troubled you?" Amy says.

He nods that indeed, the unmade bed troubled him.

She leans back, signifying a sudden change in topic. "Perhaps you could tell me about the assault that your wife—"

"Jean."

"—that your wife, Jean, suffered."

He shakes his head. "Another day."

Twenty

When Simon picked up the phone and heard, "I'm Dora Reed, Kenny's mom," two possibilities immediately occurred to him: she was calling to invite Davey to some special occasion, such as a birthday party, or there was trouble. Given recent history, more likely the latter. And so when the boy ran down the hallway Simon snared him by his shirt collar and motioned for him to stand there and wait.

"Sorry, could you repeat that, Mrs. Reed?" Davey inched toward the stairs. "Yes, I did know he took the knife to your house . . . Not beforehand, no, I learned about it when he came home. He said he forgot it was in his pocket." Davey placed one foot on the first step. "Of course we don't let him play with knives, but it's really a letter opener, with a pretty dull blade, in fact. It's not like a carving knife."

Davey waved at his father. "Tell her it couldn't cut . . ."

"They were what?" Simon stared at his son, the wild look of him, his cheek scratched, his hair sticking out, yet another rip at the neck of his T-shirt.

"No I didn't," the boy said firmly.

Simon covered the receiver. "Didn't what?"

"Whatever she says."

"I didn't know that," Simon said to Kenny's mom. "I was under the impression the knife fell out and Davey put it away immediately . . . Yes, that is a different situation."

When Simon hung up the phone, Davey was gone.

"You won't believe my new client," Amy said over her shoulder, reaching into the cabinet above the stove. Little tins and bottles were spread over the counter, along with toothpicks, muffin molds, birthday candles, matchbooks, and all manner of other small items that he rarely thought about.

Simon leaned against the sink, eating dark purple grapes one after another. He could consume the whole bunch easily. With some foods there was no limit to what one could eat. Restraint had to kick in. "Looking for something?"

"I'm rationalizing the spice cabinet."

"Rationalizing it?"

"That's what the British call organizing a space, according to a client of mine. It's the idea that a cabinet or closet has an inherent sense of reason to it that needs to be restored every so often. I like the idea."

Simon picked up a tin of cumin, opened it, and inhaled. The smell surprised him, a kind of lemony scent, or perhaps saffron, with a hint of curry. It struck him how many things there were in the world to smell, and he had sampled so few of them. He held a grape in front of her mouth, and she sucked it in. "I grounded Davey again," he said.

She nodded her agreement. "I trust you picked a good reason."

He had been prepared to explain the phone call from Mrs. Reed, Davey's lie about not taking out the knife, and his worry about their son's honesty as well as safety. But Amy was leaving it all up to him for a change. "So," he said, "what won't I believe about her?"

"Who?"

"Your new client."

Amy emptied a few flakes of spice from a bottle into the sink and washed it down the drain. "It's a *he*, actually, my first male client in two years. He's going to come twice a week. When I try to take a history he shoots off on these odd digressions. I let him go because it's the only way to learn anything. Today I asked him what he did for a living, and he said he does pretty much whatever he wants but he used to be a chamberlain."

"What's that?"

"The man who takes care of the chambers of his master, pays the bills, hires staff. Apparently it was a common position in England centuries ago, which is when he says he was a chamberlain. In 1822 to be exact."

"And he knows this how?"

"He had a reading done by a mystic of some sort who revealed his past to him."

"So he's delusional?"

Amy picked up a handful of votive candles and pushed them to the back of the cabinet. "I don't know. He's dealing with a recent loss, but there's a lot more behind it going back years. I'm not sure he's ready to seriously deal with things. I think he's playing with me."

"It's his eighty dollars, he can do what he wants for the hour, can't he?"

"The idea is that a client gathers some insight into his problems from his hour with me." Amy started putting back the spice tins, in alphabetic order. This was an odd new behavior for her—organization. He presumed it wouldn't last. "It's common for people to erect a shell around themselves to avoid talking about their problems," she said. "But this guy is doing a particularly good job of it. I think he has tremendous pain inside that he's masking with an outward hyperrationality."

"What are you going to do, wait him out?"

"I'll probably do the distracted routine, fiddle with my pen, look over his shoulder as if I'm bored with him. He's enjoying being the fascinating, mysterious stranger who baffles the therapist, so the more I seem not intrigued the more likely he is to keep coming out with things to interest me."

"Sounds like you have a game plan."

"It's not a game," Amy said, "it's a tactic. Some people need a few pokes to open them up."

Later, at the mailbox, he found another postcard, this one with a Chamber of Commerce picture of Portland Harbor on the front. The unnamed correspondent was obviously not done with his game. Simon's body tensed as he thought about what might be on the other side of the card—a new invitation? A threat? It occurred to him to just rip up the card and drop the pieces down the sewer. Nothing could compel him to pay attention except his own curiosity. He was in control.

"Hello, stranger!"

Simon looked up to see his neighbor limping toward him on the sidewalk, with large garden shears in his hands. "Hey, Bob, been a while," Simon said as he slipped the card in with the rest of the mail. "Staying ahead of the pruning, I see."

"Keeping up with it at least. That's the best I can hope for at my age." Simon backed up a step, toward his house. His neighbor took another step forward. "You found that boy of yours, I guess."

"Turns out he was in the backyard all the time," Simon said, "in the tree house."

"I figured you found him or we'd be reading about it in that paper of yours."

"Sorry, I should have called over to put your mind at ease."

Bob waved away the thought. "It's Helen who gets these ideas in her head. Thinks she hears people outside all the time. I tell her, this is Red Paint, stop worrying, but it doesn't help. Women are happiest when they have something to worry about."

Bob looked over for agreement. Simon backed up another step. "Maybe they worry too much, and we don't worry enough."

His neighbor opened and closed the shears a couple of times, as if priming them. "Doesn't matter anyway. Men are on the way out." He ran his finger along the blade of his shears.

"They are?"

"Haven't you read about it—the shrinking Y chromosome? A few thousand years, it'll be gone. Then we just get women."

A world of women brought on by the ever-diminishing Y chromosome. A peaceful world, of course, no violence allowed. "I guess we males have a few years left in us, don't we?" Simon glanced at his watch.

"I won't keep you," Bob said. "Say hello to that lovely wife of yours for me."

"I'll do that. Give my best to Helen, too."

As he walked toward his front door, Simon pulled out the postcard and turned it over. There was only one word. He stared at it for a while, as if more words would suddenly appear, magic ink activated by the light, perhaps. No more, just the one word, which he had seen before.

Twenty-one

He can't help staring at the bare arm lying on the desk, the smooth curve of the bicep, and the single blue artery on the underside of the elbow leading to a surprisingly delicate wrist. It's as if the limb has life of its own, not attached to anyone. He would like to run his fingers back and forth against the soft skin. What would be the harm?

"How are you today, Mr. Chambers?"

It is the therapist's typical opening gambit—general, imprecise, determinedly nonthreatening, a question to make it seem as if they are just two acquaintances meeting here for a friendly little chat, not a scouring of his soul. "I feel the same as always, I suppose."

"Fine," she says. But what if by *the same* he means a terrible state of existence? She should certainly explore that. "I'd like to get some background information from you before we continue. How old are you?"

"Is age meaningful?"

"It's part of an overall picture."

"Forty-two."

She writes his age down. "Are you from this area?"

"I'm not from anywhere in particular. I've moved all my life."

"Where do you live now?"

"Wherever I am. I've found that's the best way."

"It's not a philosophical question. I'm just asking for your permanent address for my records."

Name, age, address—does she think this all adds up to *an overall picture* of him? "I am where I am," Paul says. He leans up to see her note sheet, the pen poised above the empty space, waiting for him to make sense, to answer the damn question. "Does that cause you a problem, my not having a permanent address, because if it does, you can put in Truth or Consequences."

"Truth or consequences—that's a provocative response."

"New Mexico."

"Excuse me?"

"Truth or Consequences is a town in New Mexico. I thought everybody had heard of it." He watches as she writes in the name. When she finishes he says, "I've always wanted to live there."

Her head jerks up. "You don't live there?"

He shakes his head. "But I've always thought what a reminder that would be every day of your life, living in Truth or Consequences." She strikes out the name, two parallel lines. If she is an obsessive sort that black cross-out will haunt her, a blot on an otherwise clean page. Perhaps in the evening she'll redo the sheet, writing in *Unknown* for permanent address, or *Patient Refuses to Say.*

"You're not being very forthcoming with information, Mr. Chambers. I need to get to know you to help you."

"Can anyone really know another human being?" He can't believe how sappy that sounded, like the refrain to some folk lyric pretending to be meaningful.

"To a certain degree, yes, one person *can* know another. In fact, you could say that's the whole premise of therapy."

"Such a fragile foundation for one's profession," Paul says, "don't you think?" Philosophers spend whole careers parsing such a claim and come up empty. "But I am telling you all you need to know about me. You just have to listen."

She taps her free left hand on the desk, staring at him. He stares back, holding his mouth straight, restraining the involuntary smile he knows is waiting on his lips.

"How did you choose me as a therapist to contact?"

"You're in the online yellow pages. Maybe that's a mistake, advertising. Anyone can call you up. Even problem patients."

"Do you consider yourself a problem patient?"

"I'm a patient with a problem, does that make me a problem patient?"

"Not necessarily."

Paul sits up straighter. "Do you believe in consequences?" It's the type of open-ended question he prefers, leading who knows where?

"Does what I believe matter to you?"

"I wouldn't have asked the question if it didn't."

"I think we need to do more work together, and right now that means—"

"It's a basic law of physics. For every action there's a reaction—a consequence. You may believe you can act and avoid the reaction, but it will come eventually. If it doesn't, the whole universe would be disturbed."

"What exactly are we talking about here, Mr. Chambers?"

"That's funny, I'm not sure either." He shoves back his chair a little so that he can cross his legs, as a man does, his left ankle resting on his right knee, holding it there with his hand. "She was raped."

"Excuse me?"

"You asked me last time to tell you about Jean's assault. She was raped."

"I see," she says.

There it is again. Does she *see* the way Jean lay in their bed, curled toward him, but with one knee stuck out, a sentry? Her watchfulness at his every move, the approach of his hands, even the scent of him coming up behind her? Did he smell like a rapist to her, or just like any man?

"I'm struck by how you blurt out information that is obviously so important in your life. It seems you want to shock me. Am I interpreting correctly?"

"You must have seen hundreds of rape victims in your practice. I imagine it would be hard to shock you."

"I've seen *dozens* of rape victims over the years."

"They're all different, I bet. And all the same." He considers this an interesting observation.

"You told me before that your wife moved out from your apartment."

"Many times."

"Many times?"

"She moved out and then back, out and back, out and back."

Amy the Licensed Social Worker considers this information, every muscle in her face tightening just a little, the reflection of thought. "This pattern would seem to indicate that she was conflicted about staying in your marriage."

"She wasn't conflicted at all. She didn't want to live with me."

"But she kept returning."

Paul smiles in what he thinks must be an engaging way. "My magnetic personality, I suppose. I always drew her back. Until the last time, a year ago, when she moved out of state."

"Did she cut off communication with you?"

"No."

"Did you remain on friendly terms with her?"

"We were husband and wife, not friends."

"I'm asking if you remained close."

Close? They slept in separate beds, sometimes separate rooms, then separate apartments in separate states— a thousand miles between them at the end. How did Jean explain it to her friends? Was their separation something she freely admitted to everyone she met? *Yes, I do have a husband, but we're not close.* What story did she tell to make it all seem so reasonable? Was he an abuser, an alcoholic, an adulterer? She would have to say something. Probably abuser.

"Did you talk on the phone, for instance?"

Should he admit that he still speaks to her several times a day? It's a one-way conversation, of course, but he can interpret the silences, fill in the blanks. *He talks to his dog and his dead wife.* That would seem very odd to anyone reading her notes later on. He would appear delusional, which he assumes he is not, by any meaningful psychiatric definition. Of course, a delusional person can hardly be trusted judging the state of his own sanity. It's a fool's undertaking for anyone, trying to understand himself with his own prejudiced mind.

"We spoke every Sunday night," he says. Every Sunday night, nine o'clock, lying back on his bed with the phone cradled to his ear, he unzipped his pants and listened to her soft voice, turning his mouth away from the receiver. Once the phone slipped down his chest and he scrambled to pick it up with his slippery hand. She said, "Are you okay?" He coughed and said, "I'm fine."

He says, "The last time we talked was twenty-two days ago, the night before."

"What did you talk about?"

"I told her I was coming to see her."

"What did she say to that?"

"She said, 'I won't be here.'"

"What did you take that to mean?"

"That she wouldn't be there. And she wasn't—she killed herself Monday morning." Monday *morning*— why didn't he think of this before? "That's odd, isn't it, killing yourself after you just wake up?"

She hesitates, trying to appear to be the one with the answer to everything. "I don't know of any statistics on times of suicides, but it does seem unusual to wake up and take your own life."

"Jean did love her sleep," he offers as a possible reason. Some days she didn't even dress, just moved from
the bed to the couch, to the patio lounge chair, back to the
couch, and then the bed again. So much of her life hori-
zontal. Sometimes when she was sleeping he'd climb in
next to her, feel the warmth radiating into his cold body.

"You said your wife took an overdose of . . ."

"Seconals." He pictures her picking up the pill bottle, noting the dosage. What was Jean's singular emotion as she unscrewed the cap? Was she anxious or
at ease, depressed or euphoric? So much of life is one
thing or another, a dialectical world. Would the moment have passed if the cap stuck at first, childproof—
would that have given her pause?

"Did your wife leave a note?"

"That wouldn't be like Jean. She wasn't one to sum
up things. Her whole life was the note. She knew I'd
understand that."

"Do you?"

"Understand? Of course. She was raped."

"How do you know that was the reason she committed suicide twenty-five years later?"

"I lived with her for twenty of those years."

"Most rape victims carry the pain of the experience
throughout their lives, but they don't kill themselves."

"Good for them."

"I wasn't debating the legitimacy of your wife's feelings, Mr. Chambers."

"Would her suicide be any more legitimate if I told you she became pregnant from the rape?"

She looks up with interest. "Are you telling me that?"

He tips his head just slightly. Sometimes a nod can say so much more than words.

"Did she have the child?"

"No."

"An abortion?"

"No."

"What then?" As if the possibilities have been exhausted.

"She had trouble giving birth. They had to cut the baby out of her. A boy. He was born dead."

Her face twists up in a mother's expression of ache, a sympathetic response.

"Interesting way to put it," Paul says, "*born dead*. Doesn't make a lot of sense, does it."

"That's a terrible thing for a young girl to cope with."

"Jean didn't cope. She blamed herself for getting raped and then for losing the baby."

"Did you blame her for that, too?"

"I told her once, 'He ruined your life, and you ruined ours.' I'd say that's blaming her."

"Resentment is natural," she says automatically, and he wonders how often she has repeated this worthless observation. She even feels compelled to continue her point, as if sharing rare insight. "Spouses of people fighting cancer for years often get so fatigued being the caregiver that they lash out at their loved one sometimes, as if it's their fault they're sick."

What does cancer have to do with it? People die from cancer. Women live with rape. He says, "It's comforting to know that I reacted like so many other resentful spouses."

She ignores this obvious sarcasm. "Did your wife know her attacker?"

"Does that make a difference?"

"Often it does. A rape by a stranger is random, and so the victim tends to become fearful of all strangers. A rape by someone she knows can lead to fear of friends, even family and intimates."

Intimates—so that is the category in which he falls. An intimate without intimacy. "She knew him."

"Was her attacker arrested?"

"The *rapist* was never arrested. Jean never went to the police."

Her face takes on a look of recognition, eyes widening, and a slight nod. "That's quite common, unfortunately. Did your wife reveal who he was?"

"She told me who he *is*. He has a wonderful life going, it seems. Loving wife, beautiful child. Of course, you can't really tell about lives from the outside, can you? Maybe it's a cold, loveless marriage. Maybe they have a troubled little brat of a kid. I'm sure he hasn't told her about his rape. Secret lives are interesting, don't you think, how much energy it takes to keep up the illusion that you're a nice person when you know inside that you aren't?"

"Do you know where this man lives?" she asks. She has so many of her own questions to get through, and only an hour to do it.

"That's why I'm here."

She looks up at him. "The man who raped your wife lives in Red Paint?"

"Is that so surprising, a rapist in the friendliest town in Maine?"

"There are rapists everywhere, of course. Did you come here to find him?"

"No, I was just passing through and thought, *Wait a second, isn't this the place where Jean said her rapist lives? Maybe I should look the fellow up.*"

"You enjoy sarcasm, Mr. Chambers."

"I confess I do. I know it's not fashionable these days, *the humor of the weak* and all that, but it does seem to fit the question quite often."

"It fits when you're trying to deflect the question."

"I agree," he says, "I'm deflecting your question." To disarm someone, just agree. They will move on.

"What do you expect to happen when you find the man?"

"I've given up expecting a long time ago. It's a waste of time, and we only get so much of that."

"So you came to Red Paint to find the man you hold responsible for the trauma in your wife's life, and you came to me before confronting him?"

"Bad idea? Should I have just sought out the rapist directly?"

"Were you hoping I'd stop you?"

"Can you do that?"

"I think you know what I mean. Did you come to me expecting—or *hoping*, if you prefer—that I might help you find some way of coming to terms with your wife's rape and suicide that doesn't involve confronting her attacker?"

"No," Paul says, brushing lint off his pants. Where does lint come from? Does it just float in the air till a man in black pants sits down to receive it?

"Then why are you here?"

"I don't know." How could he know what God has in store? No one does, perhaps not even God. Perhaps He's winging it, like every human being on earth. We're made in His image, after all. "Maybe I should leave," Paul says as he gets up. He could hand over her fee in cash again, be gone. Better, perhaps, for both of them.

"That's up to you," she says, staying seated herself. "But whether with me or someone else, at some point you need to address the unresolved issues around your wife's life and death."

Addressing unresolved issues—is that what revenge is called these days?

"You're smiling?"

"That not allowed?"

"I'm just trying to understand your reaction."

"Don't read anything into it. I smile at inappropriate times. People tell me that all the time." She doesn't seem to smile at all herself, appropriately or inappropriately— an uncommonly serious woman.

"What would you like to achieve by confronting the man who raped your wife?"

He finds it awkward looking down at her and sits again. "I want him to confess," he says. She nods as if that is a reasonable objective, giving him a moment to expound on the subject, which he is always ready to do, any subject at all. "Did you know Martin Luther was obsessed with confessing? He'd confess for hours on end, then get up to leave, sit down again, and confess for hours more. He thought Satan had intruded into his daily thoughts."

"Do you think Satan has intruded into your daily thoughts?"

"Satan, God—it's difficult to tell who's speaking to you."

"Are you saying you hear voices?"

"I hear my own voice. Of course, I could be fooled. God can do that. Satan, too."

"What is your inner voice telling you?"

"That confession isn't really a penalty. In fact, confession can be good for the soul—it absolves the confessor. What I think is that the rapist should feel what it's like to be raped himself."

She nods again, perhaps just a habit. Surely she couldn't be endorsing the natural interpretation of his statement. What kind of therapist would do that?

"You want validation on behalf of your wife's experience," she says, "how it affected her life and yours, and you think you might achieve that by having the man who committed the rape feel some sense of what it's like."

He stares at her. So many words. Too many words.

Twenty-two

The Weekly Quotation read, "A bell cannot be unrung, but it can be smashed to bits so that it never rings again." Simon reread the quote, trying to discern if the violent image was yet another expression of his assistant Barb's post-divorce anger or, in a curious way, the beginning of her taking control of her life. The afternoon sun from the Common flooded in the large windows as he stood at his desk assessing the latest edition. The quotation, he decided, was a good sign, and he turned inside. *Police Tranquilize Black Bear on Porch* read the top headline in the Police Log on page two. Carole always led with an animal story, if one was available, and there always was. He flipped through the half pages of Religious News and Civic News and School News till he reached the Obituaries. There was just one this week, and when he saw it he couldn't stop the words coming from his lips, "What the hell?"

Jeanette Crane Walker, 41

Jeanette Crane Walker, a native of Red Paint, died of unnatural causes on June 14. Jean should be remembered for the brutal attack she suffered 25 years ago in her hometown. Her family moved away from Bowling Green Road shortly thereafter. She is survived by her husband, who will miss her eternally.　,

Jean Walker. It stunned him, the girl he knew, his graduation date, announced dead in his own paper. He pictured the last time he saw her, running up the slope toward the Bayswater Inn, holding up her long dress so she wouldn't trip. He had started to run after her but stopped because he didn't want to appear to be chasing, if anyone was looking. By the time he reached the inn she was gone.

Margaret hurried over from her desk. "Typo, boss?"

"This obit, where did it come from?"

She read it over his shoulder. "I think that's the late copy that came in Tuesday afternoon. We pulled a house ad to run it."

"Who wrote it?"

"Barbara does all the late items."

Simon looked about the newsroom, empty except for the two of them. "Where is she?"

"In the ladies', I guess." Margaret leaned against his desk. "Did you know this Jeanette Crane Walker?"

This Jeanette Crane Walker, as if she were merely a name in the paper, not flesh and blood. "Yes, I knew her. Everybody knew everybody in Red Paint twenty-five years ago."

"That must have been a big story, a brutal attack."

"No, Margaret, there wasn't any story. There wasn't any attack."

Barbara came through the back door, sipping a Diet Coke through a straw. Simon waved her over. "Where did you get the copy for this obit?"

She dropped her soda can into the metal trash basket beside his desk, and the loud noise of it jolted them all. "Sorry," she said. "What did you want to know?"

"Where did you get this obit?"

"A man came in Tuesday afternoon when you were all out back, and he had the information already written up the way he wanted it, so I rushed it in since we didn't have any other obits for the week."

"You didn't check his sources?"

She looked over to Margaret for help. "I didn't know we check sources on obits."

"That's because funeral homes send them in. This one just walked in the door. Anybody could come in and place an obit saying someone died when they haven't."

Barbara looked shocked. "You mean the woman isn't dead?"

"That's not the point. *Suffered a brutal attack*—that didn't strike you as a claim you should question?"

"Yes—I mean no, it didn't then, but it should have, yes. Should I call the police to see if they have any record of it?"

"No," Simon said, "it was twenty-five years ago. There wouldn't be any record of it. Besides, the obit has run."

Twenty-three

He runs the shower as hot as the faucet allows and rubs the fresh bar of soap over his body in long sweeps of his hand. An Irish Spring scent seeps into his skin. He stands under the blistering spray as long as he can take it and then shuts off the faucet. He dries himself, then drapes the wet towel over the curtain rod, one quarter inside, just enough to hold it on, the rest on the outside to dry. His whole self appears to him now in the full length of the door mirror. It's been so long since he's seen himself like this. His thin body has filled out over the years, rounding his shoulders, thickening his thighs. He brushes a hand slowly down his chest, following the line of dark hair to his rounded stomach, then farther down. He has a few minutes to spare.

It is a casual affair, the twenty-fifth reunion of Red
Paint High. Women in slimming black slacks and col-
ored tops. Men in Dockers pants and L.L. Bean shirts,
the same as they have been wearing for decades. Paul
comes down the broad stairway of the inn in dark
jacket and gray slacks, complemented by a modest tie,
maroon in color, asserted by a gold pin stuck in the
center. He looks prosperous and well fed, a man who
has gone off from Red Paint and done well for himself.
Just outside the dining room door stands Gus, the six-
foot-high wooden black bear in overalls, with a menu
protruding from his belly. Paul scratches under the
bear's chin, as everyone in town always did for good
luck, and enters through the double doors.

"Excuse me, have you registered?" He turns toward
a woman outfitted in the high school colors, black top
and red jacket. Her badge says Marge Francoeur,
Class Secretary. He vaguely remembers her, a thin girl
rushing down the hallways with her books clutched to
her chest. "If you've registered then just fill out a name
tag. Everyone has to have a name tag."

He imagines a world in which everyone wears his
name on his chest. It would be difficult to go unnoticed in
such a life. There are eyes everywhere now—street corners, hallways, stores, parking lots. One must assume that

at any given moment he is being watched and recorded, his behavior stored in some vast database, waiting to be retrieved when needed. It takes cunning not to be recognized. Paul takes a label and prints on it, in block letters, with a thick black pen. Then he strips off the backing and smacks the sticky paper to his lapel.

Marge leans over the table to see. *"Guess Who?*—that's a good one." She studies his face. "Bill Edison, right?"

Paul shrugs, the mysterious guest, and drifts into the sea of red-and-black balloons, red-and-black streamers, red-and-black tablecloths and napkins. He pours himself a cup of water at the folding table marked NON-ALCOHOLIC BEVERAGES and sidles into the crowd, blending in, preparing a face to greet the people that he'll meet. He is sure he won't be identified. He can be whoever he wants—a jovial sort, a studious academic, a back slapper, or his most comfortable self, the aloof observer taking it all in but not drawn in. Of this reunion but not a part of it.

By the small stage stands Simon Howe, holding forth, a shock of thick brown hair waving across his brow. So very satisfied with himself. Next to him a blond woman lingers at his shoulder, nodding animatedly at every word. Not Amy. Paul scans the room for her, at the groups of threes and fours. He thought he would have to take care not to be spotted by her, but he senses now her absence. Is it possible that she stayed home watching their son, fearful these days of leaving him alone? Simon glances over, his eyes spanning the ten steps or so between them, locks on Paul for a fleeting moment, then moves on. No recognition, just as he counted on. He slips across the room, catching bits of conversation and laughter from people who consider it great sport to make fun of their former awkward selves, forgetting how painful it was to actually be them. He sees a single man holding a plastic cup of dark liquid, and they make eye contact. The loner lofts his drink in the air, as in a toast. Paul does, too, but neither of them moves toward the other.

He turns and finds himself suddenly in a group, three women and a man. "Join us," the fellow says, "I'm outnumbered here." Paul nods and they laugh for a moment at his name tag, but no one bothers to try to figure out who he is. They assume he is a spouse, of only tangential importance to this reunion. They go around the small circle, stating their professions as if it is their identity—a mason, a receptionist, an emergency room nurse, and last, a mother of four. "All boys," she says with a sardonic tone, as if *you know how that is*.

He doesn't know and moves away from them, finds an open space by the memorabilia table stacked with yearbooks and newspaper clippings. A man wearing a red-and-black scarf draped over his shoulders pushes past Paul to the microphone and taps it. "Is this on? Can you hear me?" Everyone nods and waves. "Can I have your attention, folks? I'm Stephen Greer. In case your memory is a little shaky, I ran for class president senior year, not realizing it was a lifetime position. So here I am now, the moderator of our Red Paint High reunion." Greer clears his throat, readying himself for his speech. "Twenty-five years ago it was the best of times and the worst of times for us. We finally earned our diplomas and were ready to make our mark in the world, but at the same time we faced a terrible tragedy, the unthinkable happening to one of our own. Let's have a moment of silence in memory of our always cheerful friend, Stanley Dumas, who left the world as he lived it, at high speed." The voices in the room go silent, but behind the platform there's the sound of dishes being stacked in the kitchen and one gruntlike laugh. "All right," Greer says looking over his shoulder with annoyance, "we'll get to the dancing in a little bit, but before that we're going to take a stroll down memory lane. If you haven't submitted a question yet, there are three-by-five cards on the registration table. Write down your memories of the good old days, and do it in the form of a question. We'll see who has the best memory."

Jean did, of course, hands down. But she isn't there to play the game. Paul maneuvers his way to the cardboard table by the entrance and takes a few cards.

When the class president steps to the microphone a half hour later, Paul is standing just a few yards from

Simon. When he moves to get a drink or hug an old friend, Paul moves, too, a shadow.

"Okay, folks, give me your attention," Greer says, "I'm going to read some questions, and if you know the answer, just call it out. I'll start things off with one of my own: What did Jimmy Doyle ask Mr. Cox on his first day in physics class?"

"Why did the chicken cross the Möbius strip?" comes the call from several directions.

"And the answer?"

"To get to the same side," the voices reply.

"Right, that was Jimmy for you. Here's another one: What did Mr. Kerwin say when he picked up the ticking package in chemistry class?"

"Holy shit!" A chorus, everyone joining in, the favorite class moment of senior year.

"Right again. Let's see if we can't find a harder one." Greer shuffles the cards. "What did the National Merit Scholar get away with on graduation night?" He looks puzzled. "We had a National Merit Scholar? I didn't know that. Who was it—Sherri, Sherri Tate?" He surveys the crowd and keys in on a woman with black hair knotted halfway down her back. She shakes her head regretfully, swishing the hair side to side, her signature move, no doubt. "No?" Greer says. "Then who?"

"Simon was," comes a call from just a few feet away, the voice of the pretty blond woman standing next to him.

Greer tilts the microphone that way. "Simon Howe, the editor in chief of the finest newspaper in Red Paint, were you a National Merit Scholar?"

Simon leans out of the pocket of people where he's standing and waves. A self-effacing little gesture. So modest of him.

"Then I guess this question is about you. Want to confess what you . . ." and here Greer checks the card, ". . . *got away with on graduation night*? Something more scandalous than drinking rum and Coke in the bushes?"

Simon shrugs, retreats into his group.

"Okay," Greer says, "the next card asks, Who sneaked off to the dock during the graduation party, and what did he do there? Another graduation question. Any takers?" There are wondering glances and shaking heads. "That's a stumper. Moving on: Why didn't anyone listen when the girl on the dock . . . All right then," Greer says, slipping the cards into his jacket, "we'll stop there. Strike up the music!"

Simon leaves abruptly, weaving past the suddenly swaying bodies in the ballroom and pushing out through the heavy doors. Paul follows at a suitable distance, in the shadows of the path leading to the parking lot. He gets in the Lumina, waits till the other car starts up, then trails the red taillights onto the entrance road. He speeds up, draws closer, and turns on his brights. The car ahead slows, and he does, too. When the car speeds up again, he does also, the bright lights sweeping over it. A little farther and the car stops. After a moment Simon gets out and shakes his fist in some vague threat. Paul dims his lights for a moment, as if in apology, then turns on the brights again. Simon starts for him, but not very fast, not quite sure he should challenge whatever lies in wait for him. Paul revs his engine and hits the accelerator. *Are you watching, Jean? Am I doing this right?* The car bucks a little, then barrels down the dark, narrow road.

Twenty-four

He felt odd walking across the parking lot of the Bays-water Inn without Amy, as if there was an imbalance to him, the lack of a counterweight. And what would his classmates think? Why would he come to the re-union without his wife when they live only a few minutes from the inn?

"Simon?" came the call from behind him, and there was Holly Green coming down the gravel path, alone herself.

"Where's Steve?" he asked as she caught up.

"Home with Jenny. Where's Amy?"

"Home with Davey."

"So," she said, linking her arm in his, "we can walk in together, cause a stir."

When they reached the front door of the inn she turned toward the bay, about fifty yards down the winding drive. "I saw the obituary," she said.

"You didn't know about Jean?"

"No, we were distant cousins. We only kept in touch at Christmas. I know she got married to that guy a year behind us who was always following her around. I never understood why she did that. She said she found him a little creepy."

Voices came from the parking lot, and Simon moved Holly away from the front door into the darkness. He hoped it wasn't too obvious that he didn't want to be heard. "You drove her home on graduation night," he said just above a whisper as the voices passed them by.

"She told me she wasn't feeling well, like she was having a bad period and was embarrassed, that's why she didn't ask you."

The moon emerged from behind the clouds, and a milky light illuminated the dock. Simon was surprised at how clearly it could be seen from so far away.

"The obituary," Holly said, "it mentioned a brutal attack twenty-five years ago."

"I don't know what that was about," Simon said. He let a few moments go by for Holly to say something. When she didn't he said, "Do you?"

"Maybe it had to do with that guy. Seems like he was always pestering her that last year here. But I think she would have told me if he had actually attacked her.

Jean was a very sensitive person, like a raw nerve."
Simon hadn't thought of that description of her before,
but it seemed exactly right. The moon went under the
clouds, and he took Holly's arm again. "Shall we go in?"

"Memory lane," Simon said to Lauren, his former lab
partner in chemistry. "Next we'll be bobbing for apples
and passing an orange down the line with no hands."

She grazed his arm with hers. "Sounds like fun."
He didn't dare look at her straight on and have to answer the ever-present questions in her eyes, *Why not
me, Simon? Why not now?* He would think the answer
was obvious—he was married with an eleven-year-old
son.

"Simon Howe!" someone called from across the
ballroom. A red-haired man wearing a baseball cap
with a swordfish decal sewed on the brim pushed
through the crowd, swinging a bottle of beer from his
fingertips, just like old times. Simon recognized him
instantly, a larger-sized, bearded version of his once
best friend.

"Brewer," Simon said as he extended his hand,
"how long has it been?"

The big man ignored the hand and bear-hugged
Simon, something they would never have done as
teenagers. When he pulled away he gestured toward
the banner over the platform. "Twenty-five years, old

buddy. I haven't set foot in town since graduation. I figured I should make the effort once every twenty-five years."

"I can't believe it," Simon said, how this face that he had seen every day of his life in high school, the person he could tell anything to, was suddenly there again. "I lost track of you after you had that trouble in Portland. Where're you living now?"

"Ha Ha Bay."

It sounded like one of Brewer's jokes, but Simon didn't get it.

"It's in Newfoundland. I was sitting in a jail up in Kodiak City and all they had to read was old *National Geo*s. This story mentioned Ha Ha Bay, and I said, man, that sounds like the place for me. So when I got out I headed back across country, bought a couple acres of land up there for nothing and built myself a cabin. There's only three hundred people in town, and I figured, I can get along with three hundred people."

Strange, Simon thought, because Brewer never had a problem getting along with anyone before. It was his most positive trait. Mr. Congeniality. "So, what do you do up there?"

"Nothing, that's the beauty of the place. I made so much money fishing ten seasons in Alaska I don't need to work till who knows when, maybe never. I invested all of the money I didn't drink away. Don't you love capitalism?"

Simon did and didn't. He could see the good and the bad of it, as in everything. It wasn't a question to be answered at a high school reunion anyway. "Sounds like you've had some wild times, Brew."

"Oh yeah, but the crazy stuff gets boring after a while. I figured I'd settle down." He took a quick swig, still gripping the bottle high up on the neck. "But how about you, Simon? Putting out the old rag, I hear."

"He's owner and editor of the *Register*," Lauren said, which surprised Simon, that she was still there and part of the conversation.

Brewer looked at her for a moment like he didn't recognize her. Apparently Lauren had changed considerably since high school. "I would never have figured it," he said to Simon, "you staying in this fucking town. You were always talking about getting out first chance. I figured you'd beat me to the door."

"I did leave for a while," Simon said, an attempt at a defense. "I worked in Portland at the *Press Herald*."

Brewer emptied his bottle. "So," he said.

"So?"

"Why'd you come back?"

There was the question, plain and simple. One could always count on his old friend to ask it. Why had he returned to Red Paint? That was easy—his parents getting sick within weeks of each other and needing his care. But why did he stay after they died? That wasn't so plain and simple. He liked saving the

Register. He liked being the boss of his own paper. He liked the idea of Davey growing up where he had, in a little town in Maine, far from the temptations of the city. "Boring" actually seemed like a positive attribute back then. "You know how it is," Simon said, "you make some choices and then some more choices and suddenly you end up spending your life where you never expected."

"Yeah, like me, I never thought I'd be living on Ha Ha Bay." Brewer rolled the empty beer bottle in his hands. "You're like happy here?"

"Sure," Simon said quickly, and he wondered if it came out too fast, as if he didn't really want to think about the question. "I have a great wife and son, it's a good place to raise a family. And I like running the newspaper, so yes, I'm happy."

"That's all that counts then, isn't it? As long as you're happy." *As long as you're happy*. Despite the apparent drabness of life in Red Paint, if he had carved out some small refuge of happiness here, then great. It was nice of Brewer to grant him this. His friend took another swig of his beer. "So, how long have you two been hitched?"

It took Simon a moment to understand Brewer's inclusive glance of him and Lauren. "Oh no," he said, "this is Lauren Canelli. You remember her."

"Oh yeah," Brewer said without any remembrance in his voice, "how's it going?"

She looked past him toward the microphone.

"My wife Amy had to stay home tonight with our son," Simon said. "We've had some things going on lately, and she didn't want to leave him alone."

"Simon," Lauren said, touching his arm again, "you were a National Merit Scholar."

"Yes, why?"

"Simon was!" she called out, and it embarrassed him to hear his name shouted across the room.

On the platform, Greer pointed toward them. "Simon Howe, our editor in chief, were you a National Merit Scholar?"

He waved and nodded.

"Okay, then, I guess this question is about you. Want to confess what you got away with on graduation night?"

Simon turned up his hands and shrugged, with a little *I don't know and wouldn't tell if I did* expression. Before he turned back he glanced around the ballroom, a sweep of faces. Which one of them was accusing him?

"I'll have to get my spies investigating that one," Greer said. "The next card asks: Who sneaked off to the dock during the graduation party, and what did he do there? Another graduation question. Any takers?"

Brewer nudged him. "You ducked out early, Si."

It irritated him that his friend was remembering his high school life so assuredly. "Why would you think that?"

"They called for the king and queen to do a dance, and you weren't around, so I jumped in with Ginnie. I wouldn't forget that."

Ginnie. Why hadn't she turned up at the reunion? They could have shared a dance together now. A king needed his queen, even after twenty-five years. "I must have ducked out for a little refreshment about then," Simon said. "We all did at some point, right?"

"That all you ducked out for, old buddy?"

"Moving on," Greer said from the platform, "why didn't anyone listen when the girl on the dock . . ."

Simon felt the past jolting back into his brain—*the girl, the dock*, and the words in the obit . . . *brutal attack.*

"You okay?" Lauren touched his arm again—how many times would she do it?—squeezing a little.

He tried to smile, but he could tell by her face that his mouth was doing something else. "I guess I've had too much to drink."

"You never had the stomach for it," Brewer said.

"You need some air," Lauren said soothingly. "There's a wonderful breeze off the bay tonight."

"That sounds good." She picked her pocketbook off the chair and slung it over her shoulder. He imagined how it would look, crossing the room with Lauren, heading outside. "I don't want to drag you away," he said. "I'll just be a minute." He slipped off quickly, angling through the dancers swaying to "I Will Survive" suddenly blaring from the speakers. He swung his

186

head each way as he went, hoping to catch a gaze fixed on him. Whoever wrote those questions would certainly be watching for his reaction. So many faces—old classmates grown older, thicker, the men with beards and mustaches, the women heavier, stockier, mothers now, not the slender schoolgirls that remained in his memory. Everywhere he looked heads turned away, eyes averted.

He pushed through the double screen doors of the inn and hesitated on the porch for a moment, letting his eyes adjust to the darkness. He heard people talking on either side of him, the gravelly voices of the unrepentant smokers in the class. He hurried down the steps and headed toward the parking lot overflowing with cars angled in all directions. He found the old Corolla, climbed in, and slammed the door to make sure it wouldn't pop open at the first big bump. He swerved around the jutting front ends of much better cars and turned onto the dirt entrance road. It felt good suddenly leaving like this, telling no one. Why should he have to explain himself? Headlights appeared behind him, someone else fleeing the scene, no doubt. The lights grew bigger, coming up quickly behind him, then flashed to bright. He shielded the rearview mirror with his hand, but white light flooded his car, making the way ahead completely dark and everything that might be in his way unseeable. He slowed a little, and the follower slowed, too. He flicked his hand in a back-off gesture, but how might that appear, as a friendly wave? He slowed even more, squinting to make sure a deer or dog or even a person wasn't up ahead. He couldn't go on like this, driving blind. He stopped. The car behind stopped, too. Simon opened the door and shook his fist. That could not be misinterpreted. The lights turned down for a moment, then flashed bright again. Simon started toward the light, and it was like in a science fiction movie, the lone human moving toward the alien presence on a deserted country road. He heard the engine rev up, a screech of the wheels, and the lights came toward him. He couldn't believe this was happening. He didn't know exactly what *was* happening. He ran back to the Toyota, but there wasn't time to get in. He pressed himself against the door and closed his eyes as the vehicle rushed toward him like a furious wind.

Twenty-five

It's curious to him how relaxed he feels submitting to another human being's inspection and analysis. Maybe it is Amy Howe herself, the scent of her perfume, with its hint of citrus mellowing his brain. He has been uncommonly cooperative today. Fifteen minutes so far, and he hasn't resorted to sarcasm once.

She inhales suddenly, as if bracing herself with an extra hit of oxygen. "When you married Jean, did you know she had been raped?"

How could he miss it, just a stone's throw away, a tableau on the dock illuminated by the moon and the harsh light from the parking lot? "I saw it."

Amy's eyes widen. Apparently she can be shocked. "You witnessed Jean's attack?"

"From a distance." He knows what must be going through her mind . . . "I could have stopped Jean from being raped?"

"Is that what you think?"

A question to a question. He will add his own. "Is that what you want me to think?"

"What you think is up to you. I'm just trying to explore what that thinking is."

"My thinking is that I couldn't have stopped her being raped."

"And afterward you couldn't stop the suffering the rape caused your wife."

"That's right. I'm a failure on both counts."

"I'm not judging you, Mr. Chambers."

Of course she is. One cannot help but judge every second of one's existence. To consider is to judge.

She opens the manila folder on her desk and reads for a few moments, as if answers might be there. "When did you marry Jean?"

He notices now that she is wearing only one earring, a light blue teardrop, possibly topaz, hanging from her delicate left ear. This earring shivers a little when she moves her head. In the other ear, nothing. Is this a mistake or some new fashion? She reaches up to her right ear where he's looking, feels the absence herself, surveys her desk, and finds the missing teardrop by the phone. She sticks it back in her ear in a single quick move. *When did you marry Jean?* A change-of-pace question calculated to lower the intensity level a bit.

"After."

"After?"

"Her rape, her move from town, the loss of her baby. After everything."

"Did you marry Jean thinking that you could heal her?"

Heal her—a therapist's way of thinking, and a woman's way. "I married Jean thinking that I loved her."

"And your love wasn't enough to make her whole again?"

"Love's never enough." Paul says. "Love doesn't stop pain. Love doesn't stop hate. They say love and hate are two sides of the same coin, but that's wrong. Love and hate are on the same side of the coin, all mixed up together. Nothing separates love and hate."

"Are you saying you ended up loving *and* hating Jean?"

Of course he's saying that. Does he really need to state the obvious? Why do therapists always make you do that, as if there's no truth without words? He says, "Do you think all men are capable of rape?" Another incendiary question, blurted out. It must be considered his hallmark now. Perhaps that's how she refers to him with Simon—*my patient who blurts things out.*

He meets her eyes. They're dark green, a stirred-up sea. "I think there is the potential for violence in all people," she says, "male or female, and sometimes it expresses itself as rape."

"And before it expresses itself you can't tell who's capable of it, right? Any average ordinary guy—like an uncle or cousin or a husband, even a mild-mannered man like me, for instance—could rape, under certain circumstances." She looks up at him, sensing he has more to say. "And I did."

"You raped someone?"

"Jean."

"You raped your wife?"

The surprise in her voice surprises him. "Being married doesn't give a man license for sex on demand, does it?"

"No, but normally—"

"There was no *normally* in our marriage. Jean did everything she could to avoid sex with me."

"From the beginning of your marriage?"

"From the beginning through the middle to the end."

"I see."

He rises a bit from his seat. "Could you stop saying that? You don't see, so please stop saying it."

She hesitates, then, "I was going to say that normally—"

He doesn't care what she was going to say. "A year after we married," he says, "on our anniversary night, I decided I'd waited long enough. So I crawled on top of Jean in bed, my weight holding her down, and I spread her legs and I . . ." He can't say the word. Surely she knows what he means. "That's how I did it, maybe twice a year, no more. She didn't even fight me after the first. But each time I had sex with my wife I felt like I was raping her. *Raping her,*" he says louder.

Amy leans over her desk toward him. "Mr. Chambers?"

"*Raping her!*" he shouts.

She picks up her notepad and raps it one sharp time on the desk—"Stop!" It's so surprising, this outburst of energy from her, that he obeys. She says, "I'm afraid I'm going to have to end our session early today."

"You're afraid?"

"It's just a figure of speech. I have—"

"—other pressing business?"

". . . a family matter to attend to."

She gets up from her seat, and he does, too, a little too fast. He steadies himself with a hand on her desk. "That's a coincidence," he says, "because I have a family matter to attend to as well."

She tugs down on her blouse, a protective little gesture. "You didn't mention having family in the area," she says in a calmer voice, feeling back on safe ground, talking about families.

Paul shakes his head. "I don't. You do."

She takes a step around the desk, and he meets her there, within arm's reach, just bare space between them. She slides sideways, and he mirrors her move, as if in a dance, perfect harmony. He can't remember the last time he danced—in middle school, perhaps, some forced affair where the boys are prodded across the room toward a wall of girls a head taller, girls who giggle with their friends and shake their heads, *No, of course not, No, how could he even ask?*

"I need you to step away, Mr. Chambers." How would she deal with a patient who won't obey her command? She must have some other weapon of persuasion besides merely telling him in a stern voice to *step away.* "Are you hearing me?"

He smiles—there it is again, inappropriate without fail. He just can't help himself. He cups his ear, mockingly. "I hear you loud and clear. Do you hear me, I want to—"

"You need to move away from me right now or I'm going to call the police to remove you from my office."

Such an illogical statement. If he wouldn't move out of her way so she could leave, why would he let her call the police? He wouldn't expect such lazy thinking from her. To make the situation perfectly clear: "And if I stop you from making the call?"

"It's not going to come to that. You're going to get out of my way."

"I understand that's what you think, but if I don't, then what?" What tricks does she have up her sleeve? Mace, a hidden gun? Perhaps a silent alarm, activated already by the press of a button on her desk? Maybe in

New York, but not here in Red Paint, a friendly town, like the sign says. A village almost.

"If I call out, people will come very quickly, I assure you."

"In a perfect world, yes, people would come running from all directions to see what the matter is. But sometimes a woman screams and nobody comes."

She makes the connection quickly. "I'm sorry if that's what happened to your wife, but this session has to end right now."

"So, to recap," he says, "a grieving man comes to your office seeking help about his wife who was raped just a few miles from here. You accuse him of watching this rape and doing nothing."

"I didn't say that, I—"

"*Couldn't you have intervened, Mr. Chambers?*" he says, mimicking her probing, rhetorical voice. "*Couldn't you have pulled the rapist off, Mr. Chambers? Couldn't you have acted like a man, Mr. Chambers?*"

"You need to calm—"

"A grieving husband gets a bit angry and raises his voice," Paul says, raising his voice in time with the words. "He confides to you that he felt like a rapist every time he had sex with his wife. Your response is to end the session *right now* and call the police? I thought the goal of your profession was to help people in pain, Ms. Howe. Or do you only treat the calm and compliant sorts, the easy patients, the women?"

"I'm not debating this with you." She starts toward the phone.

Of course she wouldn't get into a debate with her client. But she might, for a moment, want to consider the unusual circumstances in which she finds herself. "You should think twice about calling the police," he says. "It could cause more trouble, and your husband wouldn't like that." Her face turns pale, and he wonders what the physiology of this reaction is, how fear works so quickly through the bloodstream. He's said the magic words—*your husband*. It's no longer just about her. Imagine if he'd said *your son*. She can't bring herself to ask the question *What about my husband?*, because that would mean she's engaging in this little scene he has created. He will continue on his own. "I'm sure you want to know what your husband has to do with this, so I'll tell you. If the police come, you'll tell your side of the story and I'll tell mine, which includes the identity of the man who raped my wife. Do you want to take a guess?"

"I don't know what you're trying to do here, but—"

"Aren't you a little curious about your husband, the rapist?" *Husband, rapist.* It must be the first time she has heard these words together. How shocking they must sound. "And once you're a rapist, you can't not be a rapist. It's a law, Aristotle's law of the excluded middle. Maybe you're familiar with it?"

She does not answer.

"No? I sense you'd be very comfortable with Aristotle. Either-or, this-that, right-wrong. No middle ground. So which is your husband, rapist or not rapist?"

She reaches for the phone, but he covers it with his right hand. She takes a quick breath and chokes on it, coughs for a few moments. Then, "I'll give you five seconds to remove yourself from my office. Five seconds."

It amuses him that she feels in the position to offer an ultimatum. He raises his left hand, spreads his fingers and counts down for her, bending his little finger first. "Of course you're curious. A smart woman like yourself, *the healer of the community.*" Then his ring finger. ". . . who learns that the man she's been married to for sixteen years raped a girl." The middle finger. ". . . and got away with it." The index finger. ". . . and hasn't paid for his sin at all." Now the thumb curls over the rest, making a fist. "Five seconds," he says. "That's all it took to tell the story of your husband's life. Sometimes there's only one fact you need to know about a person, isn't that true? Now you know that one fact about your husband." She looks at him, then away, as if he's some scary dog—a German shepherd or Doberman pinscher—that gets aggressive when challenged eye to eye. He never realized he had it in himself to appear so frightening.

"Deep down you know your husband is one of those ordinary men quite capable of rape. He wouldn't drag anyone off the sidewalk into the bushes, nothing crude like that, but he did lure a girl onto the dock by the Bayswater Inn, and he raped her. *Raped her,*" Paul says in a louder voice. "*Raped her!*" he shouts, then tilts his ear to the ceiling. "You'd think somebody would come running, like you said. How long will it take? I could yell even louder. Or maybe you want to try?" She scans the room, looking for a possible exit. The window, not a viable option, closed tight against the July heat. How would she get there, shove it up, and jump through without his calmly walking behind her and hauling her back inside, his hands wrapped around her waist? Besides, consider how hard the fall would be, ten feet down into the asphalt parking lot, a tangle of limbs twisted in unnatural directions. No, she has to stay and listen. "Then he couldn't even let her alone afterward. Your husband called the girl and told her she better keep quiet because he'd spread it all over town that she had sex with him, and that would ruin her reputation more than his."

"I don't believe you." Still a calm voice. An admirable coolness considering the situation she now finds herself in.

"There's what you believe," Paul says, "and what really happened. You can always take your pick." He removes his hand from the phone.

She grabs the receiver and punches in the numbers 911.

That's okay, he's said enough. He'll go gently now. He has another appointment to keep anyway.

Twenty-six

The postcard said: "What lies do you tell yourself about yourself? Come to the dock below the Bayswater Inn at 5:15 p.m. Thursday, alone. Faithfully yours . . ." It was leaning against the phone on his desk when he came back from lunch Monday morning. On the front was a giant moose and the caption IT'S BIGGER IN MAINE. On the message side there wasn't any stamp, meaning it had been hand-delivered by the sender himself, or maybe by some kid paid a few bucks to do it.

He would not tell Amy. This time he'd go alone.

It was an uncommonly clear day on Red Paint Bay, the kind of late afternoon where you could see across the choppy stretch of water to the cabins on the opposite shore. It looked closer than a half-mile, so close that he had tried to swim to it the night after graduation. He came down to the dock at midnight, stripped to his boxers, and jumped in. A few hundred yards out he stopped to tread water for a moment and realized that for all his effort, the lights on the other side didn't appear any nearer. He flipped over and did the backstroke to shore, staring up into the endless sky above him.

He wasn't sure this was a good idea. In fact, he figured it was probably a bad idea to come alone to the dock below the inn to meet the person sending him anonymous postcards, one of them calling him *Rapist!* He had been able in the beginning to make himself believe that the messages were meant for someone else or related to hiring David Rigero. But the obituary, the questions at the reunion, and maybe even the car nearly running him down that night swept away any pretense. The sender knew something, or thought he did, and had no doubt tracked him down to blackmail him. He wouldn't pay, of course. Acceding to blackmail would be admitting guilt, and he was innocent, at least innocent enough.

Simon heard movement behind him and turned. Crossing the beach was a man overdressed for the summer sun, in a sports jacket and tie, carrying his shoes. Simon tried to judge the stiff stride and exaggerated swing of the arms, but no name came to him to match the awkward gait. It seemed like a stranger stepping onto the dock, his heavy footsteps straining the planks. Simon suddenly felt trapped there, at the end of this narrow walkway. There was no escape but the water. Why had he let himself get into this position?

The man stopped a few feet away and nodded. He had dark hair, thinning on top, and a small clipped mustache. Yellowish skin, narrow eyes, and ears that seemed more fitting for a larger head. A face that could be easily recalled if he needed to later on.

Simon nodded back. "Sorry, but do I know you?"

The man laughed oddly in a way Simon thought he should recognize. "You bumped into me once."

"Bumped into you?"

"In the hallowed hallways of Red Paint High. My books went flying."

Simon pictured the likely scene in his head, sprinting down the narrow halls, late for class as usual, taking a corner and running over some kid, an underclassman who didn't know enough to get out of the way at final bell. "That happened a lot, as I recall. You don't hold it against me, do you?"

"You stopped and helped me pick up my books."

Simon felt relieved, which surprised him, feeling any emotion at all over such a trivial incident. "Well, I'm glad to hear I didn't just keep going." He waited a moment, allowing the conversation to proceed, but it did not. "So . . ."

The man pressed his mustache, as if making sure it was still stuck on. "I'm Paul. I was a year behind you at school."

"Paul," Simon repeated. "I don't remember any—wait, you mean Paulie, Paulie . . . Walker?"

"I'm Paul now."

Simon searched the man in front of him for a hint of the skinny kid buried in his memory but couldn't match the two images. "You delivered papers for the *Register* one year when I did, right?"

"You have a good memory."

"I just flashed on you for a second—you wore a bandanna all the time, a red one, sometimes you pulled it over your face."

"That was me."

Of all people he knew on earth, Simon couldn't think of a more unlikely person to be facing at this moment of his life. "So you're the one who's been sending me those odd postcards." It was a bit disappointing that there wasn't a more interesting person behind the mysterious correspondence. On the other hand, he felt safe finally knowing the identity of the sender, a former schoolmate, little Paulie Walker, almost a head shorter than him, not threatening at all.

"That would seem obvious."

"Right, since you're here." Simon swept his hand in

the air to create some movement to this situation. "Why?" He waited for the answer, some hint of blackmail.

"As I told you, I want to repay you for teaching me a lesson."

"What lesson is that?"

"How to keep a secret."

"A secret?"

"What you haven't even told your wife. Graduation night. You brought your date here. Jean Crane."

Simon felt his fingers tighten into fists. He felt his brain churning through recent events, forging the links. "Then you did marry Jean?"

"Another logical deduction."

He didn't like the condescending tone, or the way Paul kept staring at him, not looking away even for a moment, barely blinking. "I was sorry to read she died," Simon said.

"Jean."

"Yes, Jean. She was a very nice girl."

"She *was* a very nice girl. How easy it is to slip into the past tense."

"I just thought, since she's dead . . ."

"We'll all slip into the past tense one day," Paul said. "She *is*, she *was*. He *is*, he *was*. *Dead* is such a nondescriptive word. Why don't we just say, 'She ceases to exist'? That's all there is to it. You exist, then you cease to exist. Happens to everybody."

Simon understood now the references to mortality in the postcards. Paul had death on the brain, which wasn't a comforting thought. "Look, it's kind of hot out here for a philosophical discussion. If you want to go up to the inn, I'll buy you a drink and we can talk things over. I have a half hour before I need to be home."

Paul laughed, an irritating little sound. "You're willing to share thirty minutes of your remaining existence with me? That's very generous. But I think we'll just stay here and see how long this takes. Maybe only twenty."

"Suit yourself."

Paul set his shoes on the dock, squaring them next to each other, unnecessary precision it would seem. His socks were bunched up inside. He looked out over the water for a minute, then said, "How do you think the people of Red Paint will react when they know that the editor of their beloved *Register* got away with rape?"

Simon noted the wording—*when* they know, not *if*. Paul intended to expose him. "I didn't get away with anything."

Paul walked past Simon, brushing arms, a purposeful touch. Perhaps a provocation. He would not respond.

"This is exactly where you did it to her, isn't it?"

"Why are you asking me? You seem to know everything."

"I don't know how you could rape her."

Simon grabbed Paul's arms. "Stop saying that! I didn't do that."

"That?"

There was no communicating with this man, no use trying to reason with him. The only thing to do was get away from him as quickly as possible. "Look," Simon said, "did you bring me out here just to make a point, or do you intend to do something?"

"What I'll do I'll do," Paul said. "You'll know then. And so will I."

"That sounds like a threat. There are laws against threatening people."

"There are laws against a lot of things. That doesn't stop them from happening, does it?"

Simon couldn't disagree. "What do you want me to say, that I'm sorry what happened upset her? I am sorry. Okay?" He listened to his words, an apology on the fly, and knew it wouldn't be enough.

"*Upset* her?" Paul said. "You think being raped *upset* her?"

Simon looked out over the water for a moment, as if they were having a casual conversation and he could be distracted. "Substitute whatever word you want— *devastated*, *shattered* her. Teenagers have sex all the time and it doesn't ruin their lives."

When he looked back Paul was still staring, his

eyes fixed on him. "Jean didn't have sex all the time. She was a virgin."

"I knew that," Simon said. "She told me when we were talking about doing it."

"You talked to her about raping her?"

"We talked about having sex, Paulie. It was my first time, too."

"But you got the chance to decide when to do it. She didn't. She was a sixteen-year-old virgin."

The number jumped out at Simon—sixteen? That couldn't be right. "No, she was just a year behind me, so she had to be at least—"

"Just turned sixteen," Paul said firmly. "She skipped a grade before she moved to Red Paint. She was a barely sixteen-year-old junior who thought it was wonderful to be asked out by a senior, the captain of the wrestling team, from one of the best families in town."

"I thought she was seventeen."

"So seventeen, you wouldn't have raped her?"

"Shut the hell up!" Simon felt the anger coursing through his veins, massing for some action.

"There are laws against an eighteen-year-old having sex with a sixteen-year-old," Paul said. "It's called statutory rape. So that means it was one kind of rape or another. And you got away with both. That's a neat trick."

Rape. Statutory rape. One or the other. "It wasn't any trick," Simon said. "I told you, she never went to the police. She didn't even tell her cousin anything had happened."

"Jean kept quiet because you threatened her. She was scared."

"That's ridiculous. I didn't threaten her."

"You kept calling her."

"She was my date for graduation. I liked her. I called to find out why she wouldn't see me. When she told me I apologized—"

"You apologized for raping her?"

"Stop saying that—I didn't rape her."

"What do you call having sex with a person who doesn't want it?"

Simon threw up his hands, unable to fathom what else to say. "What do you want from me, that I go to jail for something that happened twenty-five years ago? You think you can start this whole thing up again and testify for her in court?"

"There's only one kind of justice I'm interested in— for you to tell the truth."

Simon felt better—Paul wasn't trying to get him arrested. All he wanted was the truth. That sounded simple enough. "I already told you what happened. We had sex, that's all."

"You were drunk, and you still think you know exactly what you did?"

"I know what I thought I was doing."

"That's not the same, is it?"

"You're talking as if this happened last week. I don't remember every little detail of what happened."

"Jean did, the liquor on your tongue when you kissed her. The sweat on your face. She remembered how heavy you were on her, how she couldn't open her mouth to take a breath. You smothered the words in her."

Simon remembered the way she wriggled and bucked under him, and her nails clawing down his back. For days he twisted his head over his shoulder to look in the mirror, see the long red marks of her fingernails on his shoulders. It was obvious she wanted him. He even showed Brewer. It didn't even feel like bragging then. "Look Paulie, Paul, whoever you are now, you better get yourself some serious help, because you've gone over the edge."

"I am getting help," Paul said quietly, "from a therapist right here in Red Paint. Therapists can be very understanding, especially the women. So perceptive, so hands on. I just came from seeing one, in fact. But we had a little falling out, you could say. She thinks she knows what rape is all about, but I didn't think she *really* did."

Simon grabbed Paul by the arms, held him there, inches from the water. "If you touched my wife I'll kill you."

Paul went limp in his grip, no tension at all, like a body without any life left in it. *"I'll kill you*? That's what any husband would say. You can do better than that."

Simon let go with a little shove, and Paul laughed at him. The smirking face, the accusation, or maybe it was the silly mustache, but Simon jumped on him, rode him to the dock. Then what? What do you do to a person who doesn't resist?

"This is how you like it," Paul said, breathing up into Simon's face, "being on top. You always have to be on top."

Simon sat back, like a boy in a schoolyard fight, the victor who isn't sure what he won. He got up carefully, wary of any sudden move to knock his legs out, spill him into the water. When he was clear he pulled out his cell phone and called Amy's number, watching as Paul rose to his knees, then his feet. "She better answer." The phone rang, and rang again. Then the recorded message. "Amy, where are you?" he said. "Call me if you're there, call me right away!" He turned on Paul. "Where is she?"

Paul shrugged. "You're lucky to have a beautiful wife like that."

Simon's memory triggered back to the Hall of Mirrors . . . *You're lucky to have a beautiful boy like that.* This man, Paul Walker, had been stalking Amy *and* Davey. Simon felt his fingers gather into a fist. The fist rose up and swung. Paul had to see it coming, but he didn't duck, even seemed to lean a little to catch the full weight of the punch to his face. The force of it sent him stumbling backward, over the edge. He hit the water,

sending up a wave that drenched the dock, and went
under. Simon watched the spot. A head started to break
the water, then sank again. He began counting . . . *one,
two, three*, and by *ten* it seemed like an eternity had gone
by. Why wasn't Paul surfacing? One punch couldn't
have knocked him out. Simon looked over the opposite
side of the dock, and then the far end, checking if Paul
was holding on there. *Twenty, twenty-one*—how long
could a man hold his breath underwater? Maybe he
hit his head on a rock below the surface. That would
explain the blunt trauma to his face. No one would
suspect a punch. Simon rubbed his right fist down his
shirt—no mark there, no blood on his knuckles, nothing incriminating. What was he talking about, cover-
ing up a murder? *Thirty, thirty-one* . . .

The head bobbed up, the mouth spit water and
gasped for air. Paul Walker was just a few yards from
the dock, within reach of it almost, just a couple strokes
away. His arms swatted at the water and then reached
up toward Simon. *He's drowning*. The thought of this was
surprisingly reassuring—his accuser drowning, the
man who was threatening his family drowning. Simon
turned, looked toward the inn, the small parking lot, and
around the bay, 360 degrees. Not a soul in sight. Paul's
hands were grabbing at the water now, yet his expression didn't show any fear or distress. Was this what he
wanted, to die? Would he be giving the man his wish?

The cell phone rang, *ða-ða-ða-ða,* the tone growing louder as he fumbled to pull it from his pocket. Amy.

"Simon," she said, "what's going on? Your message scared me."

"You all right?"

"I had a little problem earlier, but it's over with. What's happening with you?"

"Nothing," he said, watching Paul in the water. "I just was wondering where you were."

"I'm at the office, but I need to talk to you."

The head went under again, creating a little depression of water above it, then sank out of sight.

"Yeah, okay, but you're breaking up. I'll meet you at home later. I love you." He pressed OFF and stared into the water. It was remarkably smooth, like a sheet of dark green paper, barely a ripple of disturbance.

After some time, he couldn't say how long, Simon dove in himself.

Twenty-seven

He entered by the back door and hurried dripping over the kitchen floor to the laundry room. He unbuttoned his shirt and tossed it in the dryer. Then he undid the belt to his pants, let them fall to the floor, and stepped out of them.

"Hey, Dad, what're you doing?"

Simon whirled about and pulled his pants in front of himself, then felt self-conscious doing that. He had always tried to be easy about his nakedness in front of his son, and besides, he was still wearing boxers. He tossed the pants into the machine. "I'm just drying some clothes, Davey. They got wet."

The boy pointed at his father. "You're hairy."

"That happens as you grow older. You'll get hair on your chest, too, in a few years."

"No I won't. I'll pull every hair out."

"Good luck with that."

Davey stepped into the laundry room and boosted himself onto the washer. "How did you get so wet?"

Simon spun the dial to twenty minutes and pulled out the knob. The old dryer rattled on. "Well, I was drinking soda coming home and had to stop fast. The drink spilled all over me." The lie came easily to him, no thought needed. He just opened his mouth and there it was.

"It must have been a really huge soda."

"It was, from Burger World."

Davey reached out and poked his arm. "You shouldn't drink and drive, Dad. You could be arrested for that."

"I think I'd get off easy since it was Sprite. But you're right, I shouldn't be drinking anything. Both hands on the wheel." Simon saw his son's eyes drift downward toward his wet, clinging boxers. He grabbed a towel from the pile on the washer and began drying himself. "Let's not tell Mom about this, okay kiddo? I don't want her to worry about my getting in an accident."

"You mean you don't want her yelling at you?"

"She doesn't yell, she lectures."

"Okay, I won't tell." Davey leaned back on the washer, as if getting comfortable in a familiar chair. "Maybe."

"Maybe?"

"Then you wouldn't have to tell her about me and Kenny, would you?"

"*Kenny and me.* What'd you two do this time?'

"His mom caught us playing mumblety-peg."

"Mumblety-peg?"

"We weren't throwing at ourselves, we were just tossing his jackknife at his sister's teddy bear. If you hit him you lose."

"What is it with you and knives all of a sudden?"

"You played mumblety-peg when you were a kid, didn't you?"

Simon debated his answer. "A couple times, I guess."

"So you know, knives are cool."

"They aren't so cool when they cut you. If you don't stop playing with them I'm going to ground you for a month or however long it takes to get your attention." The boy struck the washer with his heels in a rhythm, one two, one two. Simon grabbed the legs to silence them. "Are you listening to me?"

"So we have a deal?"

It was the wrong thing to do, bargain with your kid over playing with knives. No parent in his right mind would do it. Perhaps he wasn't in his right mind, temporary insanity taking over, or more precisely, situational insanity. But how many times could he claim that? "Okay," he said, "this once, so as not to upset Mom, we'll keep our secrets."

The boy spit on his hand and held it out. "Seal it."

"I'm not spitting on my hand, Davey."

"Then the deal can be broken."

Simon lifted his hand in front of his mouth and made a spitting sound. The boy clenched their palms together, then turned them, grinding them together. Simon had forgotten this intimate adolescent ritual, how binding it really felt.

"Now we can never tell," Davey said. "Ever."

He heard her calling his name from the front door, then the pounding of her shoes as she ran up the stairs. He always found the heaviness of her step too insistent, unable to be ignored. He had hoped to be ready for her, to know what he was going to say, but here he was coming out of the bathroom with just shorts on, toweling off his head, no clue whether to tell the truth or lie. Either one had its dangers.

"Simon, are you okay?"

"Sure," he said brightly, leaning forward for their usual kiss. "Why?"

She looked at him with a disconcerted expression, thrown off by his nonchalance, or something else. "Did you just take a shower?"

"I did."

"You always take your shower in the morning before work."

He tossed the towel into the clothes hamper in the hallway. "You'll have to amend your assumptions about me," he said, with a little teasing in his voice, "because as you can see, today I showered after work."

She reached into the hamper, pulled out the towel, and took it to the bathroom. He could see her draping it over the shower rod. That was a good sign, her caring about a wet towel. She ran water and splashed it on her face, then stared at herself in the mirror. He turned away, into their bedroom.

She came in moments later and sat on the edge of the bed. "You scared me with your call," she said. "I thought something happened to you or Davey or . . . I don't know." She pulled off her shoes. "Where is he?"

"Out back," Simon said. "I saw him when I came in. He's fine. We're both fine."

"You hung up so fast, and when I called back I got your message."

"Yeah, like I told you, it was bad reception." He opened a dresser drawer and pulled out a black T-shirt.

"I had a scare today at the office," she said.

He pulled the shirt over his head, and it shrouded his eyes and ears, the world disappeared from his perception just for a moment. Then he picked up his hairbrush. In the dresser mirror he could see her behind him, watching as if there was some deep significance to his every move. He wondered how a man brushing his hair would look an hour after killing someone. What would give him away? "What kind of scare?" he said and set the brush on his bureau.

"The new patient I told you about, he wouldn't let me leave my office."

Simon felt a shiver of fear sweep over him, the same as he'd felt on the dock. Amy, trapped in her office by an insane man. She could have been assaulted or killed, and he would have been powerless to stop it. In fact he would have been the cause, bringing this lunatic upon them. He went to her, bent over her on the bed, surrounded her in his arms. She seemed smaller to him, some of the life let out of her, not the Amy he was used to. "I'm sorry," he said. "I wish I could have done something."

She made a slight wriggling motion, and he let her break free. "What could you have done?"

"I don't know. I just always think I should protect you." He looked out of the window and saw the tree house, wedged in the branching arms of the white pine, with the rope ladder dangling to the ground. The place where Davey took refuge when the stranger lingered at the front door.

"He never actually touched me," Amy said, "he just wouldn't get out of my way."

This was a usable fact—Paul holding her against her will, with who knows what intent? He could incorporate this into his story line, if one were ever needed . . . *He said he had just been with my wife in her office and implied he had done something to her . . . No, he didn't say exactly what. I imagined the worst.*

"So," Amy said, "I called the police."

Simon turned around faster than he should have. He would have to control his reactions better, not betray what was going through his mind. "Did you have to get them involved?"

"He said you wouldn't want me to."

"What?"

"My patient, Paul, he said you wouldn't like it if I called the police and he told his story to them."

His story—what would that be exactly? "I didn't say I didn't like you calling the police. I just asked if it was necessary."

"He didn't talk to them," she said, "if that's what you're worried about. He just turned around all of a sudden and left."

"Did he say where he was going?"

She looked at him curiously, still sitting on the bed, her hands in her lap, doing nothing but observing him. He realized now that it was a suspicious question. It was more difficult than he supposed to know beforehand whether a question sounded suspicious or not.

"No, he just strolled out the door like any other patient. I called back to 911 and told them there was no need to send someone, but they still had to."

Simon got down on his knees and pulled sandals from under the bed, reaching far under to retrieve the pair. When he stood up again he said, "You're not going to see him again, right?" He felt dishonest asking this, knowing what he knew. Of course she wouldn't be seeing him again. He realized at this moment that he wasn't going to tell her about meeting Paul, punching him, and watching him sink into the murky bay. She didn't need to know.

"Of course I won't see him again. He said he was leaving Red Paint anyway." Amy stared at Simon for a moment, an uncomfortable silence, as he strapped on his sandals. "He did say something very disturbing. Maybe he was just trying to shock me, I don't know, but we have to talk about it."

Simon moved toward the window again to slow down the momentum of this conversation. He saw Davey in the yard now, at the base of the tree house, gouging at the trunk with something in his hand. It had to be a knife. Even under threat of perpetual grounding, there he was in plain view carving into a tree.

"Davey's waving me to come out," Simon said. "Can we finish this later?"

"Later as in never?"

He laughed a little. "I just mean a little later. It's been a rough day."

———

After the pasta and bread sticks, after the green salad and organic mini carrots stewed in brown sugar, after watching two hours of a *Twilight Zone* marathon (Davey's choice) on television together sitting on the couch, the boy lying alternately against one and the other as if they were pillows, they sent him off to bed, and Amy said, "Is this later enough?"

Simon looked at his watch—10:05, the time they usually went up to bed themselves to read for a while. That wouldn't happen tonight. "Sure, let's talk."

"I started to tell you, I had trouble with a patient today."

"You should get some kind of security device in there," he said, "connect to the police station. I think they can do that."

"This man made an accusation, Simon. About you."

"What accusation?"

"About your graduation night on the dock by the inn. He said you forced a girl to have sex."

She was being uncommonly delicate, Simon thought. Paul would have said *rape* over and over again.

"Do you know what he's talking about?"

Simon wondered how much to say, what to include, what to leave out. There were so many ways to tell a story. "The guy you've been seeing," he began, "your patient, Paul Walker, he—"

"Paul *Walker*? He said his name was Paul Chambers."

"I think Chambers is his middle name. I guess he was using it to hide who he was. He married the girl I took to graduation, Jean Crane. I didn't really know her that well. She sat next to me in Spanish. She was pretty and smart, and since I'd just broken up with Ginnie, my steady girlfriend, I asked her to graduation. The party was at the Bayswater Inn. We ducked out a few times during the night to take a drink, me more than her, I guess. Then we went down to the bay, and things got carried away." He remembered stumbling across the sand and looking up at the moon hanging in the black sky. He remembered the hip flask concealed under his tuxedo jacket and the Chopin vodka—the finest Polish mash—that burned down his throat, like swallowing fire. He remembered twirling around, his brain spinning, the world spinning all around him.

"You had sex?" She said this in a somewhat surprised voice, as if even that was disappointing to her.

"Yes, we had sex. I could tell she was upset," he said, "after, I mean. She got her cousin, Holly Green, to drive her home. I called her the next couple of days, but she wouldn't come to the phone. Finally I went to her house and she told me that I had forced myself on her."

"Oh, Simon." He had never heard her say his name like this, with such a depth of disappointment. "I can't believe you're telling me this."

"I'd prefer not to, trust me."

GEORGE HARRAR

"You're saying you didn't force her?"

"Of course I didn't." He heard himself answer quickly and matter-of-factly. He could have let the statement stand on its own, no elaboration. What compelled him to add, "At least I don't think so"?

"You don't *think* so?"

"I had a lot to drink, and I wasn't used to it. I'd never had more than a few beers before, and this was vodka. We drank and were rolling around on the dock, and like I said, things got carried away."

"Did she say no to you?"

"She said yes, no, yes, no . . . and she was laughing. At least I thought it was laughing. I guess she was actually crying."

"There's a big difference between laughing and crying, Simon."

"No, there really isn't, not when you're drunk."

Amy leaned back on the sofa as if she was going to sink into it, then bounced forward again, on the edge of the seat. "Wait a minute, the rapist from prison."

"David? What about him?"

"Is that why you hired him, he's like a kindred spirit?"

The suggestion seemed bizarre to Simon. "That had nothing to do with hiring him. I haven't thought about Jean for years."

Amy looked at him in amazement. "I imagine she thought of you quite a lot."

"What are you trying to do, deliberately make me feel bad?"

"I'm trying to make you feel something. You tell this story like it happened to your old roommate Ray or somebody else you knew long ago."

"It did happen to someone else long ago, me as a high school senior."

"That's still you, Simon. You don't erase yourself at every stage of life. Human personalities develop in layers, one on top of the other. Scratch one layer, you can see what's below."

"Like a palimpsest."

"What?"

"A palimpsest. It's a parchment that's been over-written through the centuries, and you can still see parts of the underlying documents. If you're going to use the image, you should know the word for it."

"I don't need the word. My patients get what I mean."

"Well despite your palimpsest theory of human personality, I am different today, and I wouldn't get myself in the same situation I did twenty-five years ago."

Amy shook her head dismissively.

"What?"

"'Get myself in that same situation.' You make it sound like the circumstances happened to you."

"What do you want me to say, that I got drunk and raped my graduation date?"

"If that's what you did."

"I told you, I don't know exactly what happened. I only know what I thought I was doing at the time, which wasn't rape."

"Did you ask her if she wanted to have sex?"

"Of course. It's not like I just suddenly jumped on her."

"You asked her if she wanted to have sex with you that night?"

Simon nodded.

"Graduation night, on the dock, right before you had sex with her, you asked her if she wanted to and she said yes?"

"What are you, a goddamn lawyer? I didn't ask her at that exact moment. We talked about it beforehand."

"How much beforehand?"

"I don't know. A couple days, I guess. Sometime the week before."

"A week before? That night you didn't ask her again?"

"I asked her, as we were starting to do it."

"What did you say?"

He couldn't remember his words exactly, only the moment, on top of her. "I just said something about how we had talked about doing it and she wanted to."

"You were lying on top of her reminding her of what she said a week before?"

"You're twisting things up. It was perfectly reasonable at the time."

"The circumstances always seem reasonable to the male."

"Maybe they are reasonable. You ever consider that the guy may be reading the situation as it really is and it's the girl who gets it wrong? She misleads and flirts and sends all kinds of conflicting signals that a kid with a lot of hormones raging in him would have a hard time figuring out?"

Amy smiled in an unsmiling way. "The other side of rape."

"What?"

"Your music-loving rapist—he stood in this house in this room and told me there's always two sides to rape."

Simon hesitated, not knowing how far to go with this. But he never could back away from an argument. "Maybe there are."

"No, Simon, there are two people involved in rape, but there's only one side—the victim's. Catherine MacKinnon says—"

"Who's that?" Another name she expected him to know.

"A feminist scholar. She says the real injury of rape is what the victim perceives, but in the law it's the man's perception of what the woman wants that determines whether she's been forced to have sex or not."

"So the law's all wrong? Maybe we should have a system where a woman can claim rape even if she says beforehand she wants to have sex, acts like she wants to at the time, does have sex, but then feels guilty about it afterward. If that's the standard for rape, we better start building a lot more prisons."

"That's not what I said."

"It's what your feminist scholar said. It's all about what the woman thinks."

"It is her body."

"It's his body, too."

"Hey, what're you guys fighting about?"

Amy jumped up from the sofa. On the stairs, slouching over the railing, there was their son, in gym shorts and T-shirt, his sleeping gear. "Davey, I thought you were going to bed."

"Casper threw up on my sheets again."

Simon stood up. "If you gave her her medicine every day like you're supposed to maybe she'd stop doing it."

"That's helpful," Amy said, then turned to Davey. "Pull your sheets off and put them in the hallway. Then sleep in the guest room for tonight. The bed's made up."

"I can't sleep in there. It's like a girl's room."

"Then get new sheets from the linen closet and make your bed up yourself."

"But—"

"Do as your mother says," Simon said. "Sleep in the guest room or change your bed."

"What if . . ."

"Do it!"

Davey trudged back up the stairs, looking over his shoulder. Simon waited until he heard footsteps overhead in the hall.

"So, what, you going to treat me now like David Rigero, the social outcast?"

Amy thought for a moment, her head down. Couldn't she even look at him? Her eyes slowly raised themselves, fixed on him. "Why did you hide this from me?"

He held her gaze. "I didn't hide anything. I told you, I haven't thought about it for years."

"So you're hiding it from yourself, too?"

"Spare me the therapy, okay?"

"Maybe that's what you need, because I see this all the time. People wall off an unwanted experience in their mind. It's like an abscess that keeps growing until it bursts unless you deal with it."

"I'm not walling off anything. I don't need to dredge up something that happened in high school."

"Something you did."

"What?"

"The something didn't just happen—you did it, active voice."

"Fine, you want to parse words, here it is: I don't need to dredge up an alleged rape that I didn't do—active negative voice—a quarter century ago in order to make peace with myself or you or anyone else. Is that clear enough?"

Amy bit her lip, and it reminded him of where Davey picked up the habit. "My patient, he said you told Jean afterward that she better not spread it around that she slept with you."

"And you believed him? You think I'd do that?"

She didn't answer right away. Finally, "I want to believe you."

"You shouldn't have to *want* to."

"Don't try to make this about me, Simon. I just went through a scary session with an unstable guy who accused my husband of one of the worst acts I can think of. So I'd like to know, did you call the girl who was accusing you of rape and tell her not to talk?"

"I told you I called her because I was wondering what was going on. I finally got to talk to her for about one minute on her porch, and I tried to make her see that if this got out, everyone would know we had sex and that would be bad for both of us, maybe worse for her than me. I said I was sorry if she felt I forced her, because I honestly thought she wanted to do it."

"Apparently she didn't, because twenty-five years later she killed herself."

"Killed herself?" Simon remembered the obit—*unnatural causes*. Why hadn't he considered this before?

"That's what her husband says. An overdose of barbiturates."

"God, I thought we were just having sex, that she wanted to do it, too. I really did."

"How could you make such a serious mistake?"

Simon remembered the sting of the vodka going down his throat and how intoxicating it was to lie out on the dock at nightfall with a pretty girl in a satiny dress, her shoulders smooth and bare. It was strange, the few things one could recall from any point in time, how they had to stand in for the whole event. "I didn't want to graduate without ever having sex with a girl," he said, "and this was my last chance, the last night. Maybe I got carried away."

Her face stiffened, whatever sympathy she had started out with now drained away from it. It scared him, how ghostly she looked. "You had sex with her because you didn't want to graduate a virgin?"

It sounded despicable to him, the way she said it. "Look, we had sex like millions of kids do, and I'm embarrassed to say it took all of about two minutes. She wasn't yelling or hitting me or anything. The only way I knew something was wrong was when she ran up the hill afterward and got a ride home with Holly. She chose to make it into a horrible event for the rest of her life."

"That's what men always do in date rape—blame the victim."

"I'm not blaming her. I'm just saying she chose to be devastated."

"Did she choose to be pregnant, too?"

"What?"

"You got her pregnant, Simon. That's probably why her family left town, before she started showing."

He tried to comprehend this new information. "What happened to the baby?"

"She lost it at birth."

He didn't know what to feel—relief at not having a child he had never met or regret that some life of his, some part of himself, had died. And what must Jean have felt, having a child so young and losing it? "I'm sorry," he said. It sounded odd to him to be apologizing to Amy, but it was too late to apologize to Jean. "I didn't know any of this, obviously. She went away and I never heard from her. It didn't occur to me that she could be pregnant."

"She was, and her husband came here to confront you. It's not just a matter of strange postcards, Simon. He was getting pretty worked up in my office. I'm not sure what he might do."

"He got what he wanted scaring you. He'll go away now."

"You sound sure of that."

He was as sure as he could be that Paul Walker would not be surfacing in their lives again. He took her hands in his just like he might any time, playfully, as if he had caught her and wouldn't let go. "I don't think we need to worry."

In their bed that night, after turning out the light, he curled himself behind her as always and reached his arm over her. He would not be the one to break the routine. She didn't shake him off, and he let his body sink into her slowly, his muscles relaxing. After a moment she said, "Please don't tonight." He rolled away from her into the wide-open space of their king-size bed.

In the middle of the night he woke and thought, *It can't be true. I didn't cause another person to die.*

Yet it was true, or seemed to be. Of all things he could imagine doing in life, this had never occurred to him as a possibility. If Amy considered him so horrible as a rapist, what would she think of him as a murderer? But not murder, really. There was no premeditation. It was manslaughter at worst, or involuntary manslaughter; but not even that, just a terrible accident, a series of unfortunate events. He had even jumped in to try to save the man who had been stalking his family. Didn't that count for something?

Simon eased himself off the bed and listened for a moment. Amy was a light sleeper. Normally she would wake at any odd movement and ask if he was okay. She said nothing. He walked out of the room and down the hall in his boxers, feeling moist from the humid night air. The house was silent, nothing else stirring. He looked in on Davey, as he often did. In the dim light he could see the boy lying sideways across his narrow bed in a tangle of sheets. Casper was curled around his head. Nothing seemed changed, which felt odd to him, since everything had changed. He, Simon Howe, the editor and publisher of Red Paint's newspaper of record, had become the story himself. He imagined his mug shot, grainy black-and-white, nothing more than an accumulation of dots. He would appear disheveled, unshaven, despondent, the look of a guilty man. How many people would see him spread across the front page and say, "I'm not surprised. I knew he had it in him." The *Press Herald* would surely give it page-one coverage in Portland, a former reporter gone wrong. A writer from New York or L.A. would descend on the town and poke around like it was a newly discovered historical site. He—or *she*, perhaps, the feminine touch right for this tale of rape and murder—would become a fixture at Red's, overhearing bits of conversation, sliding her card across the counter for people to call her later and arrange a meeting at some out-of-the-way location. And they would talk, as Maine folk could once they got going, remembering stories of Simon as the talented but restless teenager, Simon as the young man who left for Portland to make his mark in journalism, Simon who ten years ago came back to buy his hometown paper, a curious move, the fallback position for a journalist who had never made it out of the state. It was obvious that he had hoped to go further. You could see it in his work. He wasn't engaged in the town the way an editor should be. Standoffish, aloof. As for the incident on the dock twenty-five years ago, there had been rumors. The girl's family left town quickly after graduation, and Simon was the last one to be with her in public. A few people put two and two together, figured something happened. Nobody said *rape*, though. Nobody went that far. But looking back . . .

Casper stirred on the bed, stood up, stretched, and sank back in the opposite direction around Davey's head. Simon turned away and tiptoed down the thickly carpeted stairs into the kitchen. If he drank tea it would be time to boil water, search through the box of odd herbal flavors, then sit with his hands cupped around the mug, breathing in the scent. All very calming. He hated tea, the thin taste of it, and the way it reminded him of being sick as a boy. Bland tea was his mother's cure for any disturbance of the stomach. He opened the refrigerator and pulled out the organic milk that Amy bought as part of her futile effort to put at least some healthy ingredients into Davey's body. Simon poured himself a glass to the very top.

It was an accident. That would be clear to everyone if he turned himself in, explained the situation, how one thing led to another. But if he had done nothing wrong, why hadn't he called the police when Paul failed to surface in the water? Why leave the scene, go home, change clothes, act as if nothing had happened? There was the sure sign that something *had* happened—acting as if it had not.

Twenty-eight

When Simon pulled into his customary parking space at the side of the Register Building facing the red brick wall, he didn't turn off the engine immediately. He sat for a moment tapping his fingers on the steering wheel, contemplating the circumstances he suddenly found himself in. He was an unrepentant rapist, according to Amy. He was the reason a woman committed suicide, according to Paul Walker. And, quite likely, he had taken another man's life, according to his own observation. Some problems had conceivable solutions. These problems seemed locked in place around him, no resolution possible. You couldn't change death back to life. Perhaps you could escape, though. He could back out of the parking space and drive out of Red Paint, out of Maine, out of his life, at least for a while. Amy would probably appreciate some time off from him. The *Register*—it could go on without him. He imagined the headline—*Editor Seen Leaving Town*. Not *Fleeing*, a concession to the fact that he did still own the paper.

The newsroom was unusually alive with activity when he finally entered the front door. Leaving town sounded adventurous, but he wasn't the type to run away. He turned toward his desk and Joe Armin materialized in front of him as he often did, as if transmitted from some other place and re-forming himself in the air. "Hey boss, big news," he said. "I heard it on the scanner—the police are over at the bay looking for a missing person."

Simon continued to his desk with deliberate speed, dropped his briefcase on the floor and picked through the mail neatly piled for him, as he would normally do. "Who's missing?"

"Some guy who was staying at the inn. They think he may have fallen into the bay and drowned."

Fallen into the bay, not pushed or punched. Simon slid his finger under the flap of an envelope and opened it. "Why do the police think somebody fell into the bay?"

"Yesterday afternoon the guy made a seven o'clock dinner reservation and said he was going down to the bay. But he didn't show up. They didn't think much of it except that this morning Ken McBride, he's the—"

"I know Ken, Joe."

"Oh yeah, right, well he found the guy's shoes and socks on the dock, so they figure maybe he was walking along there barefoot and fell in. I guess he was known for being kind of dizzy. I was going to head over there, check it out. That okay?"

It had to be okay. A reporter would naturally follow up on the possibility of a man staying at the Bayswater Inn disappearing, perhaps drowning. "Of course," Simon said. "Go get the story."

He assumed the body would be found. Red Paint Bay was no more than ten feet deep at the end of the dock, and the current there was weak. A person falling in wouldn't drift far away. As he sipped his morning coffee and scanned the out-of-town dailies, Simon tried to work out the likely sequence of events. A body would be found and identified by Ken McBride as Paul Chambers, a guest at Bayswater Inn. The evidence would point to the simple drowning of a clumsy man (the impact of small trauma to the chin would go unnoticed). An investigation would be launched into who exactly Paul Chambers was and why he was in Red Paint. The *Register* would run his picture with the caption *Do You Know This Man?* Someone, a former classmate or close friend, if he had any, would probably recognize him despite his changed appearance. They would say that he was Paul *Walker*. People would remember his being at the reunion and wonder why, since he was the year behind. Amy, feeling freed from privacy laws by her patient's death, would perhaps come forward to state that she had seen him professionally several times. It was unclear to Simon whether she would say more.

He decided to eat at Red's, his usual Friday routine, and sit at his customary spot, the red-cushioned stool at the far end of the counter. It was late for lunch in Red Paint, past one, so there were only a few customers sprinkled throughout the L-shaped diner. The waitress, Red's wife, had plenty of time to lean back against the frappé machine and catch Simon up on local gossip. "Old man Rhodes," she said, "he's on his last breaths. Doris said they'll probably put him out of his misery this weekend. It's their seventieth anniversary on Saturday. She's had her mind set on them reaching that for years, like it's some kind of record." Simon considered sending Ron over for an anniversary picture, but what would it show—a feeble old man wearing an oxygen mask and his equally old wife goading him to stay alive a little longer? People didn't want to see that. "Lenore Jenks," Red's wife said as she picked up the glass salt and pepper shakers in front of him to inspect their levels, "did you hear about her?"

"Can't say as I have." Simon scanned the menu, three pages full of fried clams and calamari, mushroom caps and mushroom burgers, pastas, curries, soups, beef and chops. Red was a versatile cook. But he couldn't spell. Simon found new mistakes every meal—the spacy chicken salad, the mazzarella sticks, and eggplant parmagiana.

"She says she knows what happened to that missing man out on the bay."

He kept his eyes on the menu, reading the nonsensical entrees, just casually interested in Lenore and what she saw. "What does she think happened?"

"She says he didn't just fall in on his own, he was pushed."

Simon thought it an appropriate time to look up, show a bit of journalistic curiosity. "How would she know that?"

"She was out walking her dog just down from the pier and she heard two men arguing, then one pushed the other. That's what she says."

Two men, that's all she apparently saw, too far away to be identified by an old woman with undoubtedly bad eyesight. All just her wild speculation. "I assume she went to the police."

"Oh sure, but she's always going over there with something she's seen, like that UFO she said was hovering over the bay last month. Like nobody else would notice a flying saucer as big as a football field."

"That is crazy," Simon said.

"Lenore's batty as hell, that's why nobody believes

her. I go visit with her twice a week, and the stories she tells. That woman could drive a saint to drink listening to her. Red says it's my penance."

"Your penance?"

"We all need to take on our fair share of suffering, and if it doesn't come to you, you need to seek it out."

"That's an interesting philosophy," Simon said, and it surprised him, coming from Red's wife. He wondered what he may have missed over the years only half-listening to her over lunch.

"It's not a philosophy," she said, "it's religion. I wouldn't do it if it were just philosophy." She reached down the counter for a water pitcher and filled his glass. "I better stop chatting before Red chews my head off. Know what you want?"

What did he want? To reclaim his life from a month ago when he was just a small-town editor of a weekly newspaper in a corner of the country most people had never visited and didn't care to. When he had a trusting wife who was smarter than he was, nicer than he was, and more honest, too. They had a high-energy boy who taxed their patience at every turn but whom they wouldn't trade for a more compliant sort. A time when no one could think of him as a rapist or killer. Unfortunately, turning back the clock was not on the vast menu at Red's Diner.

"The chowder's just made," Red's wife said, trying to prod him along. "You always like the chowder, Simon."

He didn't feel like the milky peppery soup today. He didn't really have the stomach for eating at all. But he knew it would be a mistake to start missing meals. He needed fuel to keep his mind sharp. He closed his eyes as he turned the page and when he opened them the first thing he saw was Mandarin Orange Salad. He closed the menu.

"Number twelve."

"The mandarin salad it is," she said, "but we're substituting apples today. The oranges spoiled. Nobody eats them."

"Fine, I'll have the mandarin apple salad then."

She retreated through the kitchen door, and Simon's gaze drifted toward the side window as a car pulled in, a cruiser. He turned back to the counter and cradled his water glass. He wished he had something else to do with his hands, breadsticks to eat, rolls to butter. He felt like he was in some old movie, a man on the run caught in a diner, the cops circling the place, guns drawn. It was a frightening feeling, being pursued, even if it was just a figment of his imagination. The door opened, jangling the bells, and he felt a brief rush of air sweep down the diner. His face flushed, the blood rushing to his brain, preparing him to be on guard.

"Simon, how's it going?"

He looked up into the big smiling face of Tom Garrity, Red Paint's longtime police chief. Tom always smiled, so a smile meant nothing. His blue uniform

REUNION AT RED PAINT BAY

seemed crumpled, as if he routinely slept in it. The badge
on his chest was abnormally shiny, like a child's toy.

"Hey, Tom, grab a seat."

Garrity slid his bulky leg over the adjoining stool
and shifted until he was steady, his weight evenly
distributed.

"I didn't know you dined at Red's," Simon said, a
little joke. Nobody *dined* at Red's.

"I stop in everywhere, you know. Can't play favorites."
He waved at Red's wife and made a pouring motion.

She came down the aisle grabbing a pot of coffee
and cup. "Can I get you some pie with this, Tommy?"
Red's wife was familiar with everyone. "Blueberry
today."

"No thanks," he said, patting his belly, "Peg's got
me on a diet."

He adjusted the gun on his hip, a purposeful move,
Simon thought, but for what—to assert authority? He
was probably just stopping in for coffee. Cops did that
all the time. "So," Garrity said, "how's the news game?"

"Actually it's been pretty slow this summer, Tom.
We could use a hot story."

"Maybe I have one for you. You know we're looking for a man from over at the inn who seems to be
missing."

"Yeah, I sent Joe Armin over to cover it. We'll play
the story up on page one if that helps, let people know
to keep a lookout for him."

The chief sipped his coffee. "The man's name is Paul Chambers. Know him by any chance?"

"Chambers? I don't recognize the name."

"No?"

Simon didn't like the pointed follow-up, as if the chief was offering him a second chance at telling the truth. What was he supposed to say, *You know, there was a guy I knocked into the water at the dock—I wonder if it could be this Chambers fellow you're looking for?* "Why are you asking, Tom?"

"He left a note in his room." The chief patted his jacket where the paper apparently resided. "Mentions your name."

"Really? Can I take a look?" Simon put out his hand.

Garrity looked at it. "Sorry."

Red's wife arrived with the mandarin salad, a huge plate of greens, nuts, and apple. "Anything else I can bring you?"

"This is plenty."

Garrity waited till she was out of earshot. The chief was always discreet. "Were you planning to meet anyone yesterday afternoon, Si?"

He speared a piece of apple. "I meet a lot of people every day."

"How about this guy?" The chief pulled a picture from the same pocket that he had patted before. Simon wondered what other evidence might be hidden there.

"The one in the middle," Tom said, "with the mustache. That's Paul Chambers." There was Paul Walker, standing under the TWENTY-FIFTH REUNION banner, along with a half-dozen others, arms linked, like silly old friends. He was the only one not smiling.

"If he was at the reunion I guess I saw him, that's why he seems kind of familiar. But he's not from our class, unless he's really changed a lot, including his name."

"So you don't recognize him?"

Simon tilted the chief's hand up a little to catch a better light on the picture. His brain sped through the options, running down side streets into dead ends, doubling back, trying to find the right way forward. It would be easier if he could figure out how much Garrity already knew. That would take some probing while still being evasive, what any journalist could do. "I don't understand why you're asking all these questions, Tom. What's going on?"

The chief pushed away his coffee, the cup still almost full. "We're trying to piece together what this fellow was doing in Red Paint and where he is now. It would be a great help if you could tell us anything you know."

"Like I said, he looks familiar, but with that mustache and the way his hair is, I'm not sure."

"I've got kind of a puzzle here," Garrity said. "The note he left in his room, that's about the only lead we've got."

No mention of Lenore Jenks, Simon noted. Was the chief withholding that information? "I'd like to help, Tom. Maybe if you told me what the note says . . ."

The chief thought a moment. "It says, 'Simon Howe knows the truth.'"

"That's all?"

"That's all."

"Huh," Simon said, "that's pretty bizarre." But not totally incriminating, if that really was all that Paul had written. Suggestive, certainly, hinting at a connection, but perhaps all just in his mind, a fantasy.

"He left money in the envelope to pay for what he still owed for his stay," the chief said, "so it seems he wasn't planning to come back to the inn."

Simon picked through the thicket of greens to find more pieces of apple. It was the type of thing one did to appear unfazed during the course of a conversation, act interested in something else. "You figure he was planning to commit suicide?" A comment from the side of his mouth, chewing on the apple.

"That's one possibility. But his clothes are gone from his room. And we can't locate his car."

"That is a puzzle," Simon said, and he meant it. Why had Paul cleaned out his room and moved his car prior to coming to the dock?

"So, any idea why he mentions you in the note?"

"No," Simon said, and he wondered how one should say that word, with what speed and sureness, what steadiness of gaze, how often to blink, the total expression that would make a lawman believe you. He would like to try again, with more confidence in his voice this time, no thinking necessary. "I guess the guy could have read my name on my column in the *Register*. I get crazy letters sometimes. But maybe you should talk to Amy. I didn't want to mention this, for confidentiality reasons, you know, so I can't really say that he was a patient of hers, but you should talk to her."

"He *was* a patient?"

The tenses again, always revealing, always dangerous. "He *is* missing, right, and Amy said—" Here he hesitated, as if struggling with the ethics of the situation. "—I really shouldn't be talking about him at all, you know. You've got me in a difficult position, Tom. All I can say is that Amy had a patient who gave her some trouble, on Monday I think it was. Said she called 911, so it should be in your log."

"I'll check that," the chief said as he turned his coffee mug halfway around. "And you're saying you don't know anything yourself about this guy?"

Simon gave a little shake of his head, perhaps a no, perhaps just not answering. "Talk to Amy, Tom. Maybe she can help you." Garrity stood up, took a couple of dollars from his pocket, and lay them on the counter. "You want me to run that picture for you next edition?" Simon said. "We can blow up his face, put it on page one."

Garrity hitched up his holster, which had slid below his belly. "I don't figure that will help right now."

Why would he say that? Publicity always helped in missing person cases, unless the person wasn't able to be found. Simon put out his hand. "Never know."

"That's true, I guess." The chief dropped the photo on the counter, face up.

When Simon stepped outside into the parking lot at Red's, the sun was shining brightly, as the morning weather forecast had promised, but with a few clouds hanging in the eastern sky, drifting inland, an uncommon direction for this time of year. The clouds were light on top and dark across the bottom, giving them the illusion of a solid object. He wondered if it was true what he had read, that a cumulous cloud could weigh as much as one hundred elephants. It was hard to look at clouds the same, knowing that one fact about them.

He flipped open his cell phone and dialed Amy. The call immediately kicked over to her message, as usual. He could count on it, and he often did when he didn't want to deal with her questions. "Hey Amy, it's me. Listen, I was just talking to Tom Garrity about the guy missing at the lake. It seems like it might be that client of yours you were telling me about. Tom's going to get in touch with you, I think, since I hinted that you were seeing the guy. I know you can't really say anything for

privacy reasons, right? I told Tom that. But he'll probably still try to coax something out of you. He wants to
find out where the guy is, and you don't know that, so
you can't really help anyway. Okay, this is kind of a long
message. Call me if we need to talk."

When he clicked off he wondered if he had been
clear enough—don't tell the police anything.

Joe Armin reported in by phone. "They're getting div-
ers out to search the bay," he said. "Apparently they're
checking on a report of someone falling off the dock
Monday afternoon."

Falling off—still the phrasing of an accident. Apparently Lenore was not being believed.

"Yeah," Joe said in the excited tone of a young reporter on the scene, "a counselor over at the Boy Scout
camp spotted him."

Simon's hand stiffened on the phone. It amazed him,
how hearing something threatening could instantly mani-
fest in a physical reaction, the tightening of muscles. "How
could he do that, Joe? You can't see across the bay."

"They were doing bird watching over there looking
through binoculars, so he had a good view. I think I
should go talk to him."

What were the chances that a Boy Scout counselor,
an unimpeachable observer, would be looking out into
the bay for birds and see a man fall in the water? What

else had he seen through his binoculars? And why hadn't Garrity mentioned such a credible eyewitness?

"Sure, Joe, go interview him and find out exactly what he saw."

She said, "Why did you send Tom Garrity to me?"

He was kneeling in the garden, yanking handfuls of weeds from around the spindly tomato plants, barely two feet high in July, and with only a few yellow flowers on them promising fruit. It would be another lousy year for tomatoes. He had thought that leaving work early to do something outside with his hands would help him forget for a while the predicament he was in. But there was Amy standing over him, demanding an answer.

"Hello to you, too," he said sitting back on his heels. "I suggest next year we just throw some wildflower seeds in the garden and forget trying to grow tomatoes and cucumbers. It's wasted effort."

"You do the weeding, so plant what you want." She moved away a step, letting the late afternoon sun hit his face. "Could you tell me why you sent the police chief to me?"

Simon yanked more weeds, spraying her shoes with dirt. She brushed off her shoes, lifting one foot up at a time to do it. Bits of dirt still stuck to her tan shoes like purposeful specks of contrasting color. He thought they looked interesting that way. "I saw him at Red's at lunch," Simon said, "and he started asking all these questions about the missing guy, Paul. Since you saw him a couple of times . . ."

"You're counting on me not saying anything, aren't you?"

"I know you're not supposed to talk about people you see. But I didn't think I should hold back that he was your patient since he's missing and may have committed suicide. I didn't actually say you were seeing him anyway. I implied it. I figured you'd sort things out with Tom."

"Well, he's sorting it out. Apparently once I called 911, it became a police matter."

"You mean you *can* talk about him?" Simon tried to portray only casual surprise, a kind of ethical inquisitiveness in his voice, but he was sure she could sense something more.

"I can talk about how a man who said his name is Paul Chambers prevented me from leaving my office this week, but I won't reveal anything he told me during our sessions. That's what's important to you, isn't it, that the police don't know why he was in Red Paint?"

Simon straightened a limp stalk to its pole and refixed the tie holding it. He had little hope a tomato would grow on the plant, but he thought he should give it the opportunity. In his garden, everything had its fair chance. He wiped the sweat from his face with the back of his hand. "It probably would be better if they didn't know that."

"They could get a subpoena. Then I'd have to decide what to do."

"Would you cooperate, if you were subpoenaed?"

"I might," Amy said, "if they just want information to help find him." She noticed the dirt still on her shoe and bent down to rub it away, but the dark brown just rubbed deeper into her tan sandals. "You don't want the police to find him, do you?"

He yanked a dead leaf off the stalk. "Why do you say that? Of course I hope they find him."

She shifted side to side, blocking the sun and then letting it strike him again, a strobe effect. She said, "Do you know where Paul Chambers—Paul *Walker*—is?"

He shielded his eyes to see her. "How would I know that?"

"That's not answering my question. Do you know where he is?"

Simon didn't, exactly. The last he'd seen the man he was sinking into the dark waters of the bay. Perhaps he climbed out when Simon dove under looking for him. Perhaps he floated away unseen to a different shore. Perhaps he did drown. There were several possibilities at least. Without a body, who could say he was really even dead? "No, I don't know where he is."

"Why would it take you so long to answer, Simon? You either do know or you don't."

"Like I said, I don't."

"Then why take so long to answer?"

"What are you doing, timing my answers to see if I speak fast enough for you to believe me? Is there some two-second rule I don't know about?"

"The rule is we tell each other the truth."

"Are we talking about Jean Crane again? Because I explained that to you, I didn't force her to have sex."

Amy cocked her head, adjusting to the shift in subject. "This isn't about Jean Crane. It's about her husband who came to Red Paint to get revenge on the man he thought raped the woman he married—that's you, Simon. Now he's disappeared."

"And you think I had something to do with that?"

"Did you?"

He stood up to face her, just a few feet between them. It felt good to be so much bigger. "Now you're avoiding the question," he said. "Do you think I had something to do with this guy's disappearance?"

Her eyes narrowed, trying to bore into his soul where surely the truth must lie. Souls should come with protective armor, he thought. They shouldn't be open for inspection. Four seconds, five, six . . .

"Why are *you* taking so long to answer?" he said.

"Yes."

"Yes?"

"Yes, I think you know something about him being missing."

"I can't tell you how comforting your faith in me is," Simon said. "Makes me realize how strong our marriage is after sixteen years."

"I haven't been living with a secret. I'm an open book to you. But for our whole married life you hid from me the rather important fact that a girl accused you of raping her."

"I can't believe we're having this conversation again. Apparently in your mind I'm *Simon the husband who doesn't tell his wife he's a rapist.* And now you can add to it that I'm *Simon the husband who may have done what? Killed a man?* Is that what you think?"

"I didn't say anything about you killing him, Simon." She squinted at him, as if to see more clearly. "Tell me you didn't kill him."

He would have liked to declare that he hadn't, make her feel bad for even considering the idea. But there was the nagging possibility that he may have caused the death of another human being. *Killed* him, at least in some sense of the word. With this possibility in mind, he found it incongruous to be outraged at her suspicions, but he felt outraged nevertheless. She had no good reason to think him guilty. It was her inherent distrust of him that brought her to this conclusion. A failing in her. He said, "If I tell you I didn't kill the guy or do anything else to him, you still won't believe me, will you?"

"Try me."

He turned back to the garden and dug his hands into the hard, dry dirt.

He came inside to a familiar scene: Davey sitting on the hot seat, the leather-covered stool in the family room, his feet still unable to reach the floor, with Amy circling him like a cop in an interrogation room. He wasn't needed for this performance.

"Dad!" Davey said at the sight of Simon and jumped off the stool.

Amy grabbed the boy's arm at the thin bicep and squeezed.

"That hurts," he said, twisting out of her grasp.

"Then get back on the stool. We're not done here."

Davey climbed back on.

"What's going on?" Simon said as he pulled off his work gloves.

Amy turned toward him as if addressing a jury. "It seems that your son was playing with knives at his friend Kenny's house, and according to Dora Reed, who just called, he threw a knife at her son's forearm and drew blood. She had to rush him to the emergency room for a tetanus shot. It's just a day full of good news around here."

Simon glanced at Davey, sitting behind his mother, and the boy spit on his hand and flashed it in the air. The message was clear.

Amy turned her attention back on their son. "So I'm asking you again, did you throw a knife at Kenny?"

"No, Mom, he threw it at his own stupid arm."

Amy squinted at him. "Why would he do that?"

"He was showing off how close he could get without hitting it but he missed—I mean he didn't miss, he hit himself and started bleeding. I'm the one who said he had to tell his mother to take him for a shot so he wouldn't get lockjaw. He was going to just put on his sweatshirt and not tell her. I saved his life, didn't I?"

She ignored his plea for praise. "Then why did he tell his mother you threw the knife at him?"

"He always says I do stuff that he did so he won't get in trouble because his father would kill him for something like that."

"His father isn't going to kill him."

"He'll hit him for sure, he does that all the time for the littlest little things."

"You've seen Mr. Reed hit Kenny?"

"Not exactly, but he yells a lot, I know that 'cause I heard him lots of times."

"I imagine Kenny deserves to be yelled at, just as you do more times than I can count. The point is that you and Kenny were playing with knives and he got hurt."

"No, Mom, cross my heart, I wasn't playing with knives. Dad told me not to touch them because they're dangerous. It was just Kenny doing it."

Simon watched his son's right hand crisscross his

chest, the thin index finger extended, a surprisingly delicate gesture. The boy stared up at Amy, his expression unwavering, so innocent, so convincing. Then he looked toward Simon. "You believe me, don't you, Dad?"

A clever move, trying to lure him into the scene. But Simon wouldn't let himself get drawn in. He was just an observer to this little courtroom drama where the savvy interrogator went up against the cunning suspect. Whom would the jury believe? "It doesn't matter what I think," he said, heading toward the kitchen. "It's your mother you have to convince."

That evening, Simon waited till Amy closed herself in their bathroom for a long soak in the tub, carrying a stack of *Psychology Today*s with her. She'd be an hour at least. He went to Davey's bedroom, where she had banished their son for the night on the premise that at the very least, he was on site when Kenny knifed himself. Guilt by proximity. The boy was lying on his bed, staring upward, with Casper curled on his chest. Simon turned his head up to see what was so interesting on the ceiling. Nothing. To be eleven, lying on your bed, a cat on your chest, staring at nothing. Was this to be envied or not?

"It isn't fair," the boy said, his gaze fixed upward. "Mom grounded me for not doing anything." He glanced over at Simon with his sad brown eyes and their incredibly long eyelashes. "Can't you talk to her, Dad?"

"You did do something, remember? You *were* playing with knives yesterday with Kenny."

"She doesn't know that. She shouldn't punish me for something she doesn't know I did."

"She knows, Davey, believe me. She just doesn't know she knows."

"What?"

"Never mind. When we made our pact, you didn't tell me Kenny got hurt with the knife and his mother had to take him to the hospital."

Davey grasped Casper and then rolled over, pinning the cat on her back. "You didn't ask, Dad, that's why I didn't tell you."

"Mom asked if you were playing with the knife, and you lied to her."

The boy held the back of Casper's neck with one hand and rubbed his belly with the other, a hard massage. "That's because I didn't want to get her all upset, you know, because she wouldn't understand."

The old cat twisted from side to side, trying to free herself. "Don't hold Casper that way," Simon said.

"She likes it. I do it all the time."

"You don't know she likes it, so let her go."

Davey released his grip, and Casper jumped off him and bolted toward the door.

"Why wouldn't Mom understand?" Simon said.

"She's a girl. Girls don't play with knives."

Girls don't play with knives, girls don't shoot off guns in the street, girls don't rape, girls don't murder. It seemed like a simple life to Simon, being female. He almost wished he could try it for a while. "You still shouldn't lie to her."

Davey leaned back on the bed again, his hands behind his head. "*You* lied to her."

It took a moment for Simon to process the full meaning of the words—*You, my father, the one who is supposed to teach me to be honest, lied to her.* "What do you mean?"

"When you came home all wet. You didn't really spill a soda on yourself because you'd never get *that* wet. You don't know how to lie, Dad. You try to sound like you're really really telling the truth. If you want people to believe you, you got to act like you don't care if they do."

"Seems like you've thought this out."

Davey nodded. "Yeah, lying takes some thinking ahead of time. Then you just do it."

"You sure you want to be telling me this? I am your father."

"That's okay because you lie, too. You didn't want Mom to know how you really got wet, right?"

"I didn't want her to know because—"

"It doesn't matter why, Dad," Davey said. "You lied, just like me."

It was true. He was a liar, the same as his son, and worse because his own lies were about life and death.

"Listen to me, Davey, lying doesn't solve things. It just makes them worse."

"Not if they don't catch you."

"It's not about being caught. It's what people believe. Mom doesn't believe me. She knows I lied to her."

"You lied to me, too, right?"

"Yes."

"How come, Dad? I don't care if you did something wrong."

Simon sat on the bed, his hand inches from his son's. He felt like picking it up, stroking the palm as he had done when Davey was a baby, loving the way the small fist closed over his index finger as if it would never let go. *I don't care if you did something wrong.* Not forgiveness for whatever was done, just unquestioned acceptance no matter what. One liar to another.

"You're right," Simon said, "I shouldn't have lied to you or Mom. I'm going to change that starting right now, no more lying."

Davey shifted on his side and propped his head up with one arm. "So how'd you get wet?"

"There's a man, his name is Paul, he's been sending me postcards for the last month."

"The ones on the refrigerator?"

"You know about them?"

"Yeah, since we're telling the truth, I kind of knocked the fish magnet off when I shut the door too hard and it broke on the floor. You can take it out of my allowance, if you want to." He batted his eyelashes, a feminine trait, but apparently natural in his son.

"What did you do with the postcards?"

"They're probably still on the floor next to the refrigerator."

Such a simple explanation for the disappearance of the first two cards. Nothing mysterious, nothing sinister. "The reason I lied to you about getting wet is that I was out on the dock at Bayswater Inn that afternoon with the man sending the postcards and I got into an argument with him. I thought he'd hurt Mom, and I was very upset, so I hit him and he fell into the water."

Davey rose up on the bed. "Wow, you mean that guy who's missing, you knocked him into the water?"

"That's the one. I jumped in to look for him, but I couldn't find him."

"So like he drowned?"

"I don't know for sure what happened. They haven't found him."

"Wow, Dad," Davey said again with what sounded more like excitement than worry. "They're not going to arrest you or anything, are they, because you just hit him, you didn't drown him. You even jumped in to save him, right?"

He had jumped in, dove to the bottom several times, the water so thick that he had to feel around in search of a body. Would that make a difference, his attempt at saving his victim, even if it came late?

GEORGE HARRAR

"I don't know what's going to happen, kiddo. It'll be up to the police when I tell them what I did. But people will know about it, I'm sure, and some kids might say things to you."

"Like what?"

"Things about me."

Davey balled up his small fists. "They better not or I'll punch them."

"No!" Simon said more loudly than he intended. "Aren't you listening to me? That's how I got into this trouble, punching someone. You have to be smarter than me."

"You want me to turn the other cheek?" Davey said with disdain in his voice.

That was what Simon had meant, but he realized it was useless to phrase his advice that way. "I want you to be strong enough to walk away if kids hassle you, that's what I'm telling you. Can you do that?"

"What if they keep walking after me and saying stuff about you, then can I punch them?"

"Under no circumstances are you to get into a fight over this, understand?"

"It's awful hard not punching someone who deserves it."

"I know," Simon said, "believe me."

Twenty-nine

Confessing once, Simon thought, would make the second time easier. But he didn't find it so when the second person he had to confess to was Amy. He took her hands across the small round table in the back corner of the Surf Club, Red Paint's finest fish restaurant, and most expensive. That's why there were only a few couples sprinkled throughout the dining room overlooking the Common. You could count on a secluded table at the Surf Club on a weekday.

"You proposed to me like this," she said.

Her comment confused him. "No, it was at that place on the harbor in Portland with the huge wreath made out of corks. Real classy."

"The restaurant was different, but it was candle-light like this, a seafood place, the waiter had just cleared away our plates, and you reached across the table to take my hands. I knew you had something important to say."

He remembered bringing out the engagement ring, the best $195 could buy, and trying to slip it on her. It was way too small. He couldn't believe how much he had underestimated the size of her finger. "You said yes right away, no hesitation."

"I was ready for the question. You were dropping hints for weeks."

Would she be ready tonight? Could she possibly know what he would say? "I lied to you," he said. She nodded, that was all, no other encouragement to keep him going. "I lied about Paul Walker."

She pulled her hands back from him. "Oh God, Simon, you *did* kill him?"

He wished he could say no and wipe away the fears flooding her mind, but the answer was more complicated. "I got another postcard at the office telling me to come to the dock on Thursday. Paul Walker showed up, and he started saying crazy things about Jean Crane and me. Then he said he'd just come from seeing you. He made it sound like he'd done something to you. When I couldn't get you on the phone, I figured he had."

"So . . ."

Simon took a deep breath, wondering how much truth he could bring himself to share. "So I hit him, not hard really, and he fell in the water. He was kind of flailing a little, but he was only a few feet from the dock. I figured he was all right."

"If he was that close, couldn't you have just leaned over and pulled him out?"

That had been Simon's instinct, to offer his hand. But something told him to wait a moment, to watch, to see how things went. "I wasn't sure at first what to do, so I guess I hesitated."

"You weren't sure whether to save him or not?"

"I was scared about you, so I called your cell. Then he went under again. I jumped in to find him, but he was gone. I don't know how that could be. It's not even that deep there."

Her expression changed, and he wondered if there was always this moment when her clients would notice her face seize up with the gravity of the matter. That was when they would see confirmed what they vaguely knew—there was something seriously wrong in their lives.

"I can't believe this," she said. "First I find out a woman killed herself because she felt you raped her, and now you say you knocked a man into the bay and let him drown."

"I didn't know he was going to drown. I'm not even sure he did."

"Were you hoping he would? Are you sure you didn't wish your problem would disappear into Red Paint Bay—just like Jean Crane disappeared from town?"

"God, are we back to Jean again?"

"I'm just trying to get you to understand—"

"Why is that your job? I'm not your patient. You're not the arbiter of my life. I was a goddamn horny teenager on graduation night, and you're judging me like I was fully responsible for what this woman ended up doing to herself. She had all of those years to find a way to cope with what she thought I did, and she let herself be a nonfunctioning human being and a nonfunctioning wife."

"She didn't *let herself* any more than a person with PTSD lets herself be traumatized all of her life."

"She didn't choose to get help either, did she? She took her own life twenty-five years later, Amy— twenty-five years of making herself miserable and her husband miserable and now me."

Amy cradled her wineglass in both hands. For once she was silent. For once he had the floor to himself.

"Paul Walker came here to ruin me," he said. "He didn't have to kidnap Davey or shoot me, like you thought might happen, he just had to make you think I raped her. Then he could leave town and let the story play out. He seemed like a passive guy, but he knew what he was doing."

"This isn't about him."

"You're right," he agreed quickly, "but it isn't just about me, either. It's about you, too. You're so used to sitting on your throne of morality that everything is clear-cut in your mind, all black-and-white. You took a crazy guy's account of what happened decades ago without even considering that maybe he was using me as a scapegoat, that maybe Jean was unstable for reasons that had nothing to do with me. You were sure from the beginning that I was guilty," he said, and then an unsettling thought came to him. "It's like you wanted to believe I was."

A waiter in black-and-white pushed through the kitchen door carrying a tray of desserts and walked past them without a glance.

"No," she said, "I didn't want to believe it. I don't want to believe it."

"But you can't help yourself. For some reason you're ready to think the worst about one stupid thing I did a long time ago and make it stand for my whole life."

She sipped her wine, taking her time. "Letting Paul Walker drown," she said, "that wasn't a long time ago. It was last Thursday."

She said this with a calmness that infuriated him, but she was right. It had been only a few days since he had soberly punched a man and watched him sink into Red Paint Bay. It seemed reasonable at the time, so reasonable that he couldn't say he wouldn't do it again, if Paul Walker reappeared. "He was stalking us, Amy— you, Davey, and me. Can't you understand how I felt?"

She stood up and slung her pocketbook over her shoulder. "No, I don't understand how you could let a man drown and maybe rape a girl. I don't know what to do with that information, Simon. It's just incredibly disturbing."

"So . . . ?"

"I need some time to sort things out."

Take as much time as you need occurred to him as a sensitive response, or *I'm sorry this is so hard on you.* But he didn't feel like being sensitive. He didn't care if it was hard on her. "You expect me to just sit back and give you *time to sort things out*?"

Her hand fished around in her pocketbook. He couldn't imagine what she was looking for. "That's exactly what I expect."

"Am I exiled to my office, or can I come home?"

"I don't think that would be a good idea," she said quickly.

Not a good idea *right now* or *for a while*, but open-ended, for as long as she deemed it so. Her choice. She took out two twenty-dollar bills and tossed them on the table.

He stared at the money, taking a moment to comprehend. "You're paying your half like we're on a date?" She took a step and he grabbed for her. "Amy—"

She looked down at his hand circling her forearm. "Let go of me, Simon."

"I will, but listen for a minute."

"I said let go!"

Conversations stopped at the other tables. The waiter coming out the swinging door pivoted on his heels and went back in. An elderly couple leaned into the aisle, not to miss a word.

Simon's fingers loosened their grip. "Don't do this," he whispered.

Amy shook off his hand and it swung over the edge of the table, knocking over her wineglass. Red ran across the white linen cloth. They both watched it for a moment. Then she walked away, a few quick steps to the door, and was gone. Through the front windows he saw the shadow of her get into the Volvo. He had no chance to tell her to drive carefully, as he always did.

It was the first time he had ever slept overnight at the *Register*. The old sofa in the conference room was comfortable enough, just a few inches short for him to stretch out all the way, but wide enough that he could curl on his side, his legs pulled up, the way he slept anyway. A day passed, then two. He found small reasons to call home, things that he normally took care of and she wouldn't think about. The mortgage payment was due. The painter might stop by to give an estimate on the house. She should double-check the back door at night because the lock often popped open on

GEORGE HARRAR

its own. He didn't ask to come back during these quick calls, and she didn't invite him.

The last time he phoned she said she was cooking dinner and turned the phone over to Davey. "Hey Dad," the boy said, "what's going on?"

Mom kicked me out of the house—he couldn't bring himself to say these words. There was too much to explain. "I'm staying at the office for a few days."

"Because you and Mom had a big fight, right?"

How much had she told their son? He assumed she would be charitably vague. Still, he had promised Davey the truth. "You remember when I came home wet?" Simon said. "Mom got upset when I told her how it happened."

"Told you lying's better."

Was that the lesson—lie and you get to sleep in your own bed, tell the truth and you're kicked out of the house? "Lying is what got me into this problem in the first place, Davey."

"So when are you coming home?"

Ask your mother—that's what Simon wanted to say. But he wouldn't put Davey in the middle. "It'll be a little while longer, kiddo."

"You have to come home. Mom won't let me out of her sight."

"She's just upset, Davey, hang in there."

"She's calling for dinner, Dad, gotta go."

"Love you," Simon said, just after the click on the other end.

Thirty

The postcard said TRUTH OR CONSEQUENCES, NEW MEXICO on the front, over a picture of a Western resort town nestled among the sandstone hills. Simon turned over the card and read, "The Bible says the truth will set you free. Has it? Faithfully . . ."

Paul Walker—undeniably Paul Walker. Simon looked closely at the postmark—just two days ago, three days after he had supposedly disappeared in the bay. Paulie was alive. Not drowned. Not killed.

"Good news, Mr. Howe?"

Simon looked up to see Rigero standing on the opposite side of the desk, holding a proof in his hands.

"Yes, David, very good news."

"I'm glad because I got bad news. Everything's running short on page one. We got holes all over and no copy to fill it. Meg's asking if you want to tear up the whole layout and start again."

The grin stayed on Simon's face. He couldn't get rid of it if he wanted to. *I didn't kill someone!* Gone was the threat of being interrogated, arrested, humiliated, tried, and jailed. He had nothing to hide now, especially since he had confessed to Amy. Paul Walker couldn't hurt him or his family anymore.

"Mr. Howe?"

"Yes, David, blow up page one. I'll start over after lunch."

It felt strange to Simon, turning the key to his own front door. It had only been a few days' absence, but he felt like a stranger here, a trespasser. Amy was at work—he had counted on that. Davey was gone, too, to wherever she had found for him to be while she was at work. She certainly wouldn't let him stay alone now, even during the day.

"Hello," he called from the hallway, out of habit. There was no answer.

He looked into the living room, saw the space where the old piano had been, the light rectangle remaining on the darker wood floor. He wondered what she would choose to put there—a new piano? He went upstairs, looked in Davey's room. Casper was there, as usual, curled on his pillow. She did not raise her head. There were clothes scattered about, shorts and T-shirts, as if Davey had pulled them off before bed and tossed them in whatever direction he liked—an uncharacteristic disorder.

Simon walked down the hallway to their bedroom, dragged a suitcase from under the bed, and filled it with shoes, shirts, pants, and belts. There were so few things one really needed to go out into the world.

When he went downstairs again he turned into the kitchen. The sink was full of dishes, waiting to be washed. The counter was stacked with plastic bags full of oranges, grapes, and tomatoes. Simon took the postcard from his pocket and leaned it against the or-anges, where it could not be missed.

He drove back to the *Register* faster than he should have on the narrow roads, outlining in his head the *Setting the Record Straight* column that would fill up the vacant space on page one. There was much to set straight. In the editorial room he shifted his computer away from the window, turning his back to his staff, his signal not to be disturbed. Then he began: *Dear Readers* . . .

But where to begin, how far back to go? He would confess his involvement with Jean Crane, what she thought he had done to her on graduation night—rape her—and his evasiveness to the police chief about knowing Paul Walker. He would admit to knocking his accuser off the dock and being slow to try to rescue him. He might even say that some part of him was relieved to think that the stalker of his wife and son had drowned and would not be heard from again. But what about the rest of his life, was that fair game now, too? Should he admit that he embellished his inheritance by twenty thousand dollars to secure the loan to buy the *Register*? Imagined during the abstinent last months of Amy's pregnancy what it would be like having sex with his young editorial assistant? Or that he continued smoking marijuana for years after college, even sneaking a few puffs behind the garage while Amy was inside nursing Davey? If the truth set one free, why not confess it all? In a lifetime there were so many weaknesses and deceptions one inevitably succumbed to. He was sure he was just scratching the surface remembering them. What would all of these indiscretions add up to, anyway? Nothing remarkable. In the end he was sure his sins were pretty ordinary. Except one, perhaps.

In the crowded paste-up room, amid stacks of unsold copies of the *Register* dating back years, David Rigero fit the last strip of copy onto page one, the two left columns. He stepped back and admired his work. "You did it, boss, no more empty space."

Simon leaned forward to read The Weekly Quotation: *"We live amid surfaces, and the true art of life is to skate well on them." —Emerson.* Barbara had chosen well this week, an observation that seemed to fit him perfectly. He did skim the surface—Amy told him that once—but he didn't think it was necessarily a bad way to live. There was art to skating well, even to just staying on your feet. It was certainly better than cracking through the ice and sinking into dark, frigid waters.

"Pretty funny, isn't it, Mr. Howe?"

Simon looked up, trying to make the connection to the Emerson quotation. "How do you mean?"

"You and me in the same boat—people thinking we're rapists."

"Funny is one word for it."

"It takes balls putting this in, telling people everything. Or stupidity, if you don't mind my saying so."

"Stupidity may be more accurate."

Rigero flexed his arms, bulging his biceps for a moment, and it surprised Simon that they didn't seem very big. "Don't you have a priest or someone you could confess to? It would save you a lot of trouble."

"There's no tradition of confession in my church," Simon said.

"Too bad. A few Hail Marys and Our Fathers, you're clean."

The idea that a few repetitions of words could clear one's soul seemed bizarre to Simon. Surely one had to do more than confess in private.

"I could still yank this out," Rigero said, "plug the space with a house ad."

"We don't run house ads on page one, David, and I'm not changing my mind anyway. It feels good getting everything out there—nothing to hide anymore, nothing to explain. Everybody should do it once in their lives."

"It's your funeral," Rigero said as he took his roller and pressed the copy firmly in place. He peeled the page off the makeup table and held it up. "That's a wrap, boss. Want to go for a beer?"

Simon imagined what Amy would say if she knew—two supposed rapists going for a beer together. She'd be furious. "Sure, David," he said, "why not?"

Thirty-one

The crescent moon cast a thin light over Red Paint Bay, barely enough to reveal the narrow arc of sand curving toward the dock. The white Toyota that sputtered into the dirt parking lot pulled up to the barrier rocks, then went silent. Inside Simon stared through the blurry windshield as if expecting something to happen—fireworks, a meteor shower, or perhaps some miraculous visitation.

He opened the door, swung his legs out, and leaned down to pull off his sneakers and socks. He walked across the small beach, digging his toes into the sand with each step. The feel of the grains reminded him of the first day each summer when he was a kid and could go without shoes. Running out the back door, down the winding path that led to the water, then hours of exploring the edges of the bay till his face burned from the sun and his tender feet were cut and bloody.

He picked up a handful of sand and let it slide through his fingers. He watched for a minute as the water lapped onshore in miniature waves. A half mile across, the opposite side was dotted with pinpricks of illumination, like fallen stars. He walked out onto the dock and a spark of light caught his eye, a firefly writing in the darkness as if on a blackboard. That was odd, a solitary beetle weaving its distinctive pattern so far away from the tall grass where potential mates could see the display. As a boy he'd watch them for hours in his backyard, fireflies by the hundreds flickering off and on. One night he snatched one from the air, proving to himself how quick his reflexes were. It shocked him when he opened his hand to see the mangled legs and wings, and he quickly wiped his palms down his pants.

There was laughter from the inn, and he turned instinctively to look up the hill. He wondered at how easily sound traveled, how much could be heard. He pulled his T-shirt over his head and ran off the end like a broad jumper, his legs pumping to keep himself airborne. It was only seconds, but time enough to imagine himself eight years old again, wanting more than anything to light up like a firefly. When he hit the water, it swallowed him whole, a giant mouth. He let himself sink straight down until his feet touched the spongy bottom. The muck of the bay surrounded his legs, holding him down.

After some time, he couldn't imagine how long, the air burst from his lungs. He flexed his knees and shoved upward, his hands stretched out as if grabbing for the rungs of a ladder. The water above him seemed endless. He wondered if he had miscalculated and was really going sideways. Maybe the beers had disoriented him. He tried to hold his lips shut, but the brackish water seeped in. When his head finally broke the surface, he lifted his mouth toward the sky and coughed and spit.

He swept his hands in and out, treading water. He figured he could stay afloat like this for hours if he needed to, plenty of time to think. The *Register* would come out Thursday morning, as usual. The citizens of Red Paint would read all about him, reveling in the intimate details of a life turned inside out in front of their eyes. They would judge him, of course, split for and against, but with a certain reluctance, realizing that it could well be any one of them being judged. Davey would hear comments about his father, taunts perhaps, and he wouldn't be able to stop himself from getting into fights. He would find the whole thing proof that telling the truth didn't make sense when a lie could make life so much easier. Amy would latch onto the abundant shame of the matter, make it hers.

After a while, she would try to work through her disappointment in him, seeking her way to a grudging
acceptance. And he, Simon Howe, what would become
of him? Perhaps the truth *would* set him free, as Paul
Walker suggested, but from what—memory, guilt,
Amy? Could he bear her grudging acceptance? There
was no way to know what lay around the next corner,
what new entanglements, what new possibilities. He
would just have to show up for his life as he always
did and see what happened, since there was no other
good option anyway. He sank a few inches, letting the
waters of Red Paint Bay rise to just below his eyes.